Angel Bob

By Iain Grant

Illustrated by Giuseppa Barresi

Pigeon Park Press

Paperback ISBN: 978-0-9927034-9-3

Published by Pigeon Park Press

www.pigeonparkpress.com
info@pigeonparkpress.com

Cover and interior created by and copyright © Giuseppa Barresi – www.ryuuza.co.uk

<u>Dedication</u>

To Georgie, Ethan and Ella, who laughed in all the right places.

1 – Myrtle and Belinda

Myrtle Green's best friend was a chicken called Belinda.

There were six chickens living at the bottom of Myrtle's garden. Belinda was the biggest of the six chickens, was the first out of the coop in the morning and the last to go in to roost at night. Belinda was a tall, proud bird with white feathers all over except for a few black feathers in her wings. Myrtle thought Belinda was quite beautiful and Myrtle loved her.

And yet, each night, when Myrtle went down to the chicken coop to put all the chickens to bed, she thought about what it meant to have a chicken as your best friend. What it really meant was that Myrtle didn't have any real friends, friends who were children, not chickens, and this thought made Myrtle a little sad. She could feel the sadness inside her, like a little round stone in her belly. The little lump of sadness didn't hurt. It just sat there and it didn't seem to want to go away.

Myrtle had once had some real friends, when she was smaller. Back then, the whole family, Myrtle and her mum and her dad, had lived together on a farm in the countryside. They had kept cows and pigs and chickens and there were ducks on the pond and an old horse in the meadow. The children who lived on other farms nearby had been her friends. Most of them were older than her but that didn't matter. They played hide and seek around the cowsheds. They ate picnics and played adventure games in the fields. They visited the horse in the meadow and sometimes fed the ducks on the pond.

That was a long time ago, at least in Myrtle's mind. One day, Myrtle and her mum had to leave the farm for good. They had to move to the town and move in with Nanna who had a house that was much smaller than the house on the farm. The cows and pigs and the horse and most of the chickens went to other farms and only six of the chickens came with Myrtle and her mum to the new house. Myrtle didn't see any of the children she used to play with after they moved. Now, she couldn't remember what some of them truly looked like and she had forgotten most of their names.

Myrtle went to a new school in the town. Her teacher was kind and Myrtle didn't dislike the other children in her class and Myrtle herself was perfectly pleasant but, somehow, things had become very different for Myrtle and she wasn't sure how she could ever make friends amongst these new children.

And so that was how Myrtle came to have a chicken for a best friend.

Every morning before breakfast, Myrtle would get up, get dressed and go out into the garden to see the chickens. The chickens had a solid wooden coop and a large run that was covered in wire and, each morning, Myrtle would let the chickens out of the coop and into the run and then make sure they had plenty of food in their feeder and plenty of fresh water in their water tray. She would collect their eggs (Belinda's were always the largest) and

6

then go back into the house to wash her hands and have her breakfast.

Every afternoon, after school, Myrtle would go straight to the chicken run to check that they were all right and ask Belinda what kind of a day she had had. Belinda never answered. She just clucked sometimes. Then, when night fell, Myrtle would come out again and put the chickens to bed, locking them carefully into their coop so that the foxes couldn't get at them. Foxes love to eat chickens and will dig a tunnel under any fence if they think there might be a tasty chicken on the other side. Mr McAndrew, who lived up the road and who grew carrots and leeks and radishes on the allotments just beyond Myrtle's back garden had told Myrtle that a family of foxes lived thereabouts. Myrtle had never seen one of the foxes but was determined not to let them come anywhere near her chickens.

One night, Myrtle came out into the garden to put the chickens to bed. Normally, once it was dark, the chickens would have already taken themselves into their coop, fluttered onto their perch and be waiting quietly, but that night Myrtle could hear a constant clucking sound coming from them. Fearing that a fox might be about, Myrtle sprinted down the dark garden to the coop.

Myrtle found no fox at the bottom of the garden nor any sign that one had been near. Five of the chickens were nestled up in the coop as usual but Belinda was stood in the very centre of the run, looking up into the night sky and clucking in a worried manner.

Myrtle put her hands on her hips as she had seen her mum do so many times before and said in her most exasperated voice, "What *is* the matter with you, Belinda?"

Belinda paid her no attention at all. She simply went on clucking with her shiny little eyes raised to the sky. Myrtle looked up. The stars were out above. In the town, the stars were hardly ever as bright as they had been at the farm but tonight they were large and shining silvery blue. They looked close enough to reach out and touch, close enough to snatch out of the air.

"Wow," said Myrtle. "I've never seen them so bright. Have you?"

Suddenly she saw a glint of moving light, flying across the blackness and curving slowly towards the ground. A shooting star!

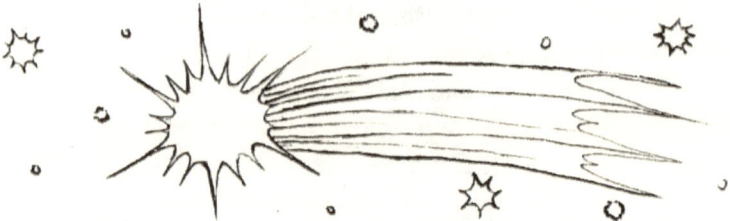

"Make a wish, Belinda. Quickly! Shooting stars don't last long."

Myrtle closed her eyes tightly and wished with all her heart. When she opened her eyes the shooting star was still there. It was larger, closer now and moving faster above them. Since it had not yet disappeared, Myrtle thought it would be okay to make another wish. She screwed her eyes shut and made a second silent wish.

When she opened her eyes again, the shooting star was still there and seemed to be very near, very near indeed. Myrtle couldn't be sure but it now looked like a bird, an enormous bird made of burning white light, spinning around and lighting up the whole garden. It didn't look very much like a star anymore.

Myrtle ducked. Belinda gave an almighty squawk of terror. The shooting star, or whatever it was, whistled past them at great speed and shot over the fence at the bottom of the garden. The garden was abruptly dark once more.

Myrtle looked at Belinda. Belinda looked at Myrtle. Belinda's terrified eyes were as large as saucers.

"What was that?" said Myrtle.

Myrtle dashed over to the fence and looked between two fence slats at the allotments on the other side. The allotments were pitch black but for a flickering white glow of light not far from Mr McAndrew's allotment patch. Myrtle squinted hard to try and see better. She wondered if the little flickering light was just Mr McAndrew in his potting shed, having a late night cup of tea but Myrtle told herself that it couldn't be. The light was on the ground and definitely not coming from any potting shed.

"It's landed in the allotments, Belinda," whispered Myrtle. Myrtle was excited and just a little afraid. She knew that real shooting stars hardly ever came down to earth and they certainly didn't glow once they had landed. Myrtle had no idea what the thing in the allotments could be but despite being a teensy bit scared she was determined to find out.

"I'm going to go and have a look at it," she told Belinda.

Just then something brushed by Myrtle's cheek. It was a feather, floating gently down towards the ground. Myrtle caught it. It was as white as a snowflake and as long as Myrtle's hand.

It was not a chicken feather.

2 – The Allotments

Getting from the back garden to the allotments was not that easy. There was a gate to one side of the garden which led out onto a little side road. A short way down the road was another gate. This gate was wide and had tall iron railings and beyond it laid the allotments.

Myrtle was not allowed out on her own after school and would certainly get into trouble if found wandering the streets at night. But she also very much wanted to go and look at the thing that had fallen into the allotments and so she crept over to the garden gate and lifted the latch.

Before she went out, Myrtle looked up the garden at the house to see if she was being watched by her mum or Nanna. There was a light on in the kitchen window and another behind the closed curtains of Nanna's bedroom. Myrtle was sure that if her mum or Nanna had seen the falling star they would have been outside in a flash but there was no sign of either of them. Nanna would be sat up in bed, reading one of those thick novels about poor women from olden times she loved so much. Myrtle's mum would be sat in the living room watching boring soap operas on TV with the sound turned up high.

No one will notice if I'm gone for a few minutes, thought Myrtle and slipped quietly out through the gate.

There were no streetlights in the little side road but the brilliant stars above cast enough light for Myrtle to see her way by. It was only a minute's walk to the allotments but in the strange, shadowy night the short journey seemed to take forever. The peculiar outlines of hedges and trees loomed out at her and each shadow made Myrtle's heart flutter. The air was cool and smelled of rain.

Myrtle knew that the gate to the allotments was locked most nights with a padlock and a length of chain so she was relieved to find that no one had locked up yet. She pushed the gate open a little and squeezed through.

It took a moment for Myrtle to see where the shooting star, or whatever it was, lay. It was glowing feebly on the ground not far from Mr McAndrew's vegetable patch. There were several allotments between the gate and the glowing thing and Myrtle had to pick her way carefully between plants and tools and other things she couldn't make out in the dark before she got to where the glowing thing had landed.

When she was close enough to see it properly, Myrtle stopped and stared in surprise. The glowing thing was, well it was... a boy!

The boy was sat on the ground in the middle of a patch of cabbages, looking very dazed, a bit confused and more than a little worried. He had a pale face, sparkling blue eyes and curly golden hair that was almost as long as Myrtle's. The light that Myrtle had been seeing – and this was very strange – seemed to be coming from around and behind the boy's head as though someone were stood behind him shining a torch at the back of his head, although there was no such person here.

Forgetting her manners, Myrtle said, "How do you do that?"

The boy stared at Myrtle.

"The light," said Myrtle. "How do you do that?"

"Where am I?" said the boy.

"The allotments," Myrtle replied. "You've squashed quite a few cabbages there. Someone will be very cross in the morning when they see this."

This made the little boy look even more worried and Myrtle suddenly felt sorry for him. She reached out a hand to him and helped pull him to his feet. The boy was wearing a white gown, which now had quite a few muddy brown and cabbagey green stains on it.

"I shouldn't be here," he said.

"Neither should I," said Myrtle. "I'll be in big trouble if my mum finds out. Was it really you I saw falling from the sky?"

The boy nodded.

"Did you hurt yourself?"

Before the boy could answer, the door of a nearby potting shed was opened and a skinny old man with a scraggly beard stepped out, a torch in his hand.

"Mr McAndrew!" Myrtle whispered to the boy. "I thought he'd gone home."

"Who's out there?" Mr McAndrew shouted. "Don't think I didn't hear you, you wee toerags."

He shone the torch here and there, swinging it back and forth as he looked for them.

"We've got to go," Myrtle whispered. She grabbed the boy's hand and led him away quickly. The beam of Mr McAndrew's torch followed them but never quite managed to find them, even though Myrtle tripped over a watering can and the boy almost got tangled up in some runner bean poles as they ran. They reached the gate and squeezed through.

Across the night air, Myrtle heard Mr McAndrew mutter to himself, "Blasted foxes!" Then there was the sound of Mr McAndrew slamming his shed door shut and, finally, there was silence.

"That was close," panted Myrtle. "Come on."

"Where are you taking me?" asked the boy.

"My house, I guess," said Myrtle.

They walked back up the road to Myrtle's house, hand in hand. Myrtle couldn't stop herself staring at the boy and the weird light that shone around his head.

"You're not from round here, are you?" she said thoughtfully as she opened the gate leading back into her garden.

"No," said the boy sadly. "I'm a long way from home."

3 – An Angel in the Garage

Belinda clucked at Myrtle and the boy as they entered the garden. The boy jumped in surprise, clutching his hands to his mouth.

"Don't worry," smiled Myrtle. "It's only Belinda."

"Who's Belinda?"

"My chicken. One of my chickens. And I need to put her to bed."

Myrtle nipped into the chicken run, shooed Belinda into the coop where the other chickens were waiting and locked the door.

"Is that *your* house?" said the boy.

"No, silly," said Myrtle, coming out of the run. "*That's* my house." And she pointed up the garden to the tall thin house where lights were still shining in the kitchen and in Nanna's bedroom window and, thankfully, there was no sign of anyone having noticed that Myrtle had been out of the garden. "Do you have anywhere to go? To stay, I mean," asked Myrtle.

The boy shook his head. Myrtle sighed.

"Mum will go crazy if she discovers I've been out of the garden at night," she said. "Can't take you in the house but… I guess I can find somewhere for you to sleep for the night."

15

Together they went up the garden but, instead of going into the house, Myrtle took the boy round the side and through the little door into the garage.

"We don't have a car, so there's plenty of room," said Myrtle. "Let me find the light switch."

Myrtle felt around the wall, brushing aside ancient cobwebs with her fingers, until she found the light switch. Blinking at the sudden glare of the dusty hanging bulb, Myrtle turned to the boy.

"It's a bit fusty in here but it's dry and-"

She stopped and gawped in disbelief at the boy. Strange he might have seemed, with that glow hovering about his head and the fact that he had fallen from the sky into the allotments but now Myrtle saw something stranger still.

"You have wings!" she gasped.

Myrtle had not noticed them outside in the night time gloom for they were the same pure white colour as the boy's gown and she had perhaps mistaken them for bulges in his clothing but now she could see them clearly. The boy's wings were beautiful things that arched out from his shoulders like white feathery rainbows.

Myrtle took from her pocket the white feather that she had caught out of the air earlier.

"Then this is one of yours," she said.

"Yes," said the boy. "I bashed my wing against something as I fell. I think I've damaged it."

The boy stretched out his wings and then winced in sudden pain.

"Oh, my. You're an angel," said Myrtle.

"Yes," said the boy.

Myrtle stretched out a finger and prodded him in the chest.

"A real one."

"Yes."

At that precise time there were a thousand different questions buzzing around inside Myrtle's head, hundreds of whats and whys and wheres and whos and hows, but there were so many that she couldn't utter one of them.

In the end, she said, "This is amazing! When I saw you in the sky I thought you were a shooting star!"

"Oh," said the angel.

"I made a wish on you!"

The angel looked around the garage, at the dirty concrete floor, the shelves packed high with boxes and old tins of paint, the bundles of rags stuffed in the corner.

"Is it all right, I mean is it safe for me to stay here?" he asked. "I won't be able to fly again until I've rested my wing."

"Of course," said Myrtle. "There's my old tent and sleeping bag over here. Look. You can lay the tent out on the floor and sleep in the sleeping bag on top. Do you want anything to eat? Do angels eat?"

"Yes, we do," said the angel, "but I'm not hungry, thank you."

There came a shout from outside.

17

"Myrtle! Are you *still* out there?"

"That's my mum!" Myrtle exclaimed. "She can't find you here!"

"Why not?" said the angel.

"Because," said Myrtle. "We don't get many angels round here. And it's not normal. And things that aren't normal make grown ups freak out. It's the law, or something. No, you stay here. I've got to go in."

"I understand," said the angel.

Myrtle went to the door.

"I can't believe you're real," she said. "You will stay here, won't you? Don't leave in the night without saying goodbye, please."

The angel looked at the sleeping bag laid out on the floor.

"I won't," he said. "It looks really comfortable here," he added politely.

"And maybe your wing will be better by morning."

"Maybe."

"Myrtle!" came Mrs Green's shout. "Where are you?"

"Well, goodnight then," said Myrtle.

"What did you wish for?" said the angel abruptly as Myrtle reached for the light switch.

"I'm sorry?" said Myrtle.

"When you thought I was a shooting star," said the angel. "What did you wish for?"

Myrtle hesitated, a little embarrassed.

"A friend," she said quietly and turned off the light.

Myrtle went out to her mum who was waiting impatiently on the doorstep to the kitchen.

"What have you been up to?" said Mrs Green.

"Just looking at the stars," said Myrtle. "They're very bright tonight."

Together they went inside. Myrtle took herself upstairs, brushed her teeth and got into her pyjamas. She then went into her Nanna's room to give the old lady a kiss goodnight and then finally returned to her own room and climbed into bed.

18

Myrtle laid beneath the sheets, staring at the ceiling for a long time, the angel's discarded feather tucked beneath her pillow. A little voice in her head was saying over and over again, "There's an angel in the garage. A real, live angel. Sleeping in *my* garage," and she worried that the garage might be too cold or too draughty or too spooky for the angel to rest in properly. All the while, rolling around her insides was a bubbling mass of excitement and joy which, although Myrtle did not realise, had completely washed away the small lump of sadness she had been carrying around in her belly for so long.

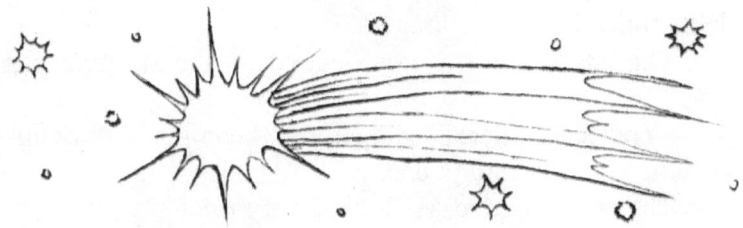

4 – The Celestial City

The following morning, Myrtle awoke slowly from the most weird and wonderful dreams. She yawned, stretched and, rolling over, put a hand under her pillow. Her fingertips touched the feather she had placed there the night before and she remembered that her weird and wonderful dreams weren't dreams at all: there was an angel sleeping in the garage.

Myrtle leapt out of bed, throwing her sheets halfway across the room in her excitement. Forgetting slippers and dressing gown, she pelted down the stairs and into the kitchen. Mrs Green was at the kitchen sink, doing the washing up. Nanna was at the breakfast table, eating a soft boiled egg with toast.

"Good morning," said Mrs Green.

"Morning, ducky," said Nanna.

"Morning, mum. Morning, Nanna," Myrtle panted breathlessly as she opened the back door.

She was about to dash out when her mum thrust an empty egg box in front of her face.

"Don't forget this."

Myrtle stared at it for a moment and then remembered herself. She had to go let the chickens out, feed and water them and collect their eggs first. Snatching the egg box from her mum, Myrtle dashed outside and ran barefooted down the damp, dewy lawn to see to the chickens.

There were four eggs that morning. The one Belinda had laid weighed twice as much as any of the others. Myrtle put them in the egg box and then carefully ran back up the garden with them. Her mum wasn't stood by the kitchen window so Myrtle was able to slip unnoticed into the garage.

The angel was sat cross-legged on the sleeping bag on the floor.

"You're still here!" said Myrtle, beaming with delight. "You said you would be and you are."

The angel nodded. He looked very tired.

"Did you get any sleep?" asked Myrtle.

"Not much," said the angel.

"Was it too uncomfortable? Or too cold? I hope the spiders didn't disturb you."

"No," said the angel. "It's just so strange being here I couldn't sleep. And my wing hurts."

The angel spread his right wing out to show Myrtle although doing just that seemed to cause him some pain. Myrtle could see that the wing seemed a little twisted at one point and a few of the feathers were wonky and out of place.

"You need a bandage on that," she said. "I'll fetch one."

Myrtle went out from the garage and into the kitchen. Nanna was still at the table struggling with her breakfast. Mrs Green was not around but Myrtle could hear her moving about upstairs. Myrtle placed the egg box on the kitchen surface and went to the cupboard next to the sink to look for the first aid kit. The cupboard was untidy and there were boxes of this and packets of that stacked higgledy-piggledy inside, which made it very hard to find anything at all.

"What are you looking for, ducky?" asked Nanna.

"Nothing, Nanna," said Myrtle.

"Then you've already found it, haven't you?" Nanna chuckled.

"Actually, I'm looking for the first aid kit. I've got to bandage a wing."

"Ah, then you'll need to look under that tub of plant seeds," said Nanna. "That one there. That's right."

Myrtle pulled out the first aid kit and closed the cupboard door.

"Thanks, Nanna," she said and then, grabbing three slices of toast out of the rack on the breakfast table, went out to garage again.

"I've brought you something to eat," said Myrtle, passing the toast to the angel. "Sorry it's not buttered."

The angel bit into a slice and chewed hungrily.

"It's smashing. Really delicious," he said as though he was eating the most wonderful thing in the world ever. "What's it called?"

"Er, toast," said Myrtle.

"Toast!" said the angel, spitting crumbs. "Smashing!"

Myrtle took a bandage from the first aid kit and went round behind the angel to look at his poorly wing. Myrtle didn't know much about medicine and certainly knew nothing about treating damaged angel wings but she guessed that if she wrapped it up so that it could not move too much then it would heal all the quicker. So, Myrtle set to work on binding up the wing, apologising every time she made the angel flinch with pain.

Soon she had finished bandaging the wing and used a safety pin to fix the bandage in place. She sat down beside the angel whilst he finished his toast. As the angel ate it seemed to Myrtle, who was watching him very closely, that the weak light that glowed around his head was becoming brighter, stronger with each mouthful he ate.

"What is that?" she asked.

"Hrmm?" said the angel, his mouth full of food.

"The light on your head."

"It's my halo," said the angel. "I know mine's not very big. Most of my brothers' are enormous. They're as bright as the sun. Well, nearly."

"Your brothers?" said Myrtle.

"The other angels," he explained and then his face suddenly became very sad. "They told me not to come here. They told me not to get too close."

"Too close?"

"To the Earth. They warned me but I only wanted to look."

"Have you not been on Earth before?" asked Myrtle.

23

"No," said the angel. "We're not allowed. We can't interfere with things anymore. We're supposed to leave people alone and let them sort out their own problems. But I wanted to come and look, to see your magical little world up close. There are so many amazing things in this world of yours: mountains and lakes and jungles and birds and animals and fishes and creepy-crawlies and plants and trees and… and toast! Do you eat toast often?"

"Every day," said Myrtle.

"Wow! It's really great!"

"It's just toast."

"Yes, I know but we don't have toast back home," said the angel.

"Where is your home… exactly?" asked Myrtle.

"The Celestial City," the angel replied. "It's where all the angels live. It's really beautiful. Silver and glass and gold. It catches the light of a thousand stars and every tower and every spire of the city gleams with that light. The city is the brightest thing in all the heavens."

"It sounds fantastic," said Myrtle.

"Yes," said the angel, "but we don't have toast there."

Myrtle thought for a moment or two.

"So, if the Celeslis… Cecily…"

"Celestial."

"If the Celestial City is the brightest thing in the heavens, does that mean we can see it from Earth?"

"Oh, yes," said the angel. "Although it will look just like a bright star from here."

"Then tonight, when it's dark, you could point it out to me. I would really love to see it."

The little angel suddenly burst into tears, shaking his head.

"What's the matter?" said Myrtle, taking the angel's hand in hers.

"I can't," he sobbed.

"Can't what?"

"Can't show it to you." He sniffed back his tears. "I don't know anymore."

"Why not?" said Myrtle.

24

"I...I flew all the way here from the Celestial City. I knew exactly where I was going and I was sure I knew the way back. For a long time I hovered above the Earth at a safe distance, just watching it go by beneath me. Have you ever seen the forests and the deserts and the seas from a hundred miles up?"

"Er, no."

"They're so pretty," said the angel. "I could have stayed there and watched the world turn for a year and a day and I wouldn't have been bored. I should have stayed there. But I was greedy and I wanted to see more so I came down a little closer and then a little more and then a little more. And then, out of nowhere, this big metal box with a dish on it comes flying at me and knocks me out of the sky."

"A big metal box...? You mean a satellite?" said Myrtle.

"I don't know what it was but it hurt," said the angel. "I fell down, spinning round and round so much that I couldn't tell up from down. That's when you must have spotted me. I came down to the ground with such a bump. And when I looked up" – the angel gave a little sob – "I realised that I had been spun around so much that I couldn't work out which of the stars in the sky was my home."

Myrtle dabbed at the angel's tears with a tissue she had found in her pocket.

"There, there. Don't worry. Let's not give up just yet. You will need to rest your wing for a few days. Maybe in that time we can find out which star is the Celestial City."

"You think so?" said the sniffly angel.

"Definitely," said Myrtle.

"And I can stay here?"

"As long as you like."

"Thank you."

"That's okay," said Myrtle. "I've got to get ready for school now but I'll be back later on this afternoon. You'll be all right in here until then."

The angel nodded.

Myrtle picked up the first aid kit and went to the door.

"By the way," she said, "my name's Myrtle."

"Hello, Myrtle," said the angel.

"And what's your name?" she asked.

"I can't tell you," said the angel.

"Why not? Were you spun around so much that you forgot that too?"

"No. I haven't forgotten it. I just can't say it to you. Angel names are powerful and wondrous things which people were never meant to hear. If I told you my name, you would laugh and cry at the same time and not be able to stop for hours."

"Really?" said Myrtle, surprised. "Isn't there an angel called Gabriel and another called Michael. Those names don't make me want to laugh and cry at the same time."

"That's because they're not their real names. The Archangel Gabriel's real name is so wondrous that it would make your head explode. Gabriel is just the name that people have given to him."

"Then we'll have to think of a name to give to you," said Myrtle. "Something for you to think about today. See you later."

Myrtle left the garage and went inside the house to get dressed for school.

5 – Isaac's Telescope

It's very hard to concentrate at school when you know that there's an angel living in your garage. Somehow, an angel seems more important than practising long division, more important than learning about how people lived in the Middle Ages and much more important than carrying out experiments with magnets. Myrtle found it very difficult to focus on her schoolwork that morning and didn't even realise that her teacher, Miss Gordon, was talking to her until Miss Gordon slapped her ruler on the desk and shouted her name.

Myrtle sat bolt upright.

"Yes, Miss?"

"Get your head out of the clouds, little miss daydreamer."

There were a few unkind sniggers from Myrtle's classmates.

"Yes, Miss," said Myrtle timidly.

"Now, I'll ask again, what answer did you get for question five?"

Myrtle looked at the work in her maths book. She hadn't even got up to question five and she could see that the children around her had completed all ten questions that Miss Gordon had asked them to do. Myrtle sighed. Miss Gordon was not going to be happy.

Later, at break time, after a very unpleasant morning in the classroom, Myrtle wandered alone around the playground. She found a bench to sit on beneath a shady tree and wondered what the angel was doing at that moment. She imagined that he would be very bored sat on his own in the garage. Perhaps she ought to have taken some toys or books out to him. She couldn't think of anything in the dusty old garage that could provide any entertainment.

A group of boys was standing near to Myrtle's bench, talking about football and telly and the other things boys talk about. Myrtle wasn't deliberately listening to their conversation but one of them, Ryan Roberts, who was one of the children who had sniggered when Miss Gordon told Myrtle off, said something that made Myrtle prick up her ears.

"I was watching the footie with my dad, round at his place," said Ryan, "International match on satellite telly. It was nil-nil and there was only five minutes to go and, suddenly, the TV went all fuzzy."

"That happened to our TV too," said another boy. "But we were watching a film on satellite television."

"Well, none of the satellite TV stations were working after that," said Ryan. "My dad says he's going to ask for his money back. He says he's not going to pay for satellite telly if the satellite isn't working."

Myrtle swallowed hard and thought back to what the angel had said about the 'metal box' which had knocked him out of the sky. Had the angel been hit by a TV satellite and had it been damaged when the two of them crashed together? If it had then someone else besides her might know that something had fallen to Earth last night.

At that, another boy said, "Maybe it has something to do with the meteorite that came down yesterday."

This comment came from Isaac Adelman. Isaac was also in Myrtle's class. He was podgy, asthmatic and had about as many friends as Myrtle did.

"Meteorite?" said Ryan.

"I saw it with my telescope," said Isaac

Myrtle's throat went dry. Someone *had* seen the angel fall to Earth.

"Telescope? You have a telescope?" sneered Ryan. "You're such a nerd, Isaac!"

The group of boys laughed and jeered at Ryan's cruel comments. Isaac lowered his head and walked away, humiliated.

28

Myrtle got up and scurried after Isaac.

"Wait!" she called out. "Isaac, wait!"

"Leave me alone," he said hotly.

"No, wait," she said. "Did you really see him, I mean it, fall to the ground?"

"What if I did?" said Isaac. The unkindness of the other boys had made him angry and suspicious.

"I... I thought I saw something last night too," said Myrtle. "Whilst feeding my chickens. Did you, by any chance, see where it landed?"

"No," said Isaac, "but I'm sure it landed somewhere near the town. My uncle – he's the one who bought me the telescope – says that scientists will be coming to look for it."

"What will they be looking for?" said Myrtle.

"The meteor. A piece of rock from space."

"And if they don't find it?"

Isaac frowned at Myrtle.

"Why wouldn't they find it?" he asked. "Do you know something that you're not telling me?"

"No," said Myrtle. The lie felt hot and uncomfortable in her throat.

A teacher stepped into the playground and rang the bell for the end of break time. Quickly, gratefully, Myrtle slipped away to join the queue to go back inside.

29

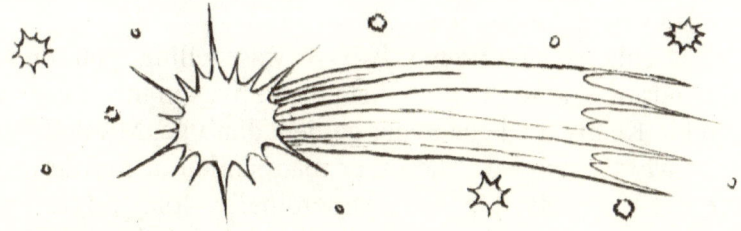

6 – The Scientist

As soon as the end of day school bell rang, Myrtle was out of her chair and charging towards the door. She had spent the whole afternoon fretting and worrying about the angel, about how he was coping all alone in that garage and what would happen if some people did really come looking for him and she was desperate to get home to check he was okay. With her book bag swinging at her side and her lunch box held tightly under her arm, Myrtle ran out of the school building, through the gates and up the road towards her home.

She had to wait for the lollipop lady at the one road she needed to cross. Myrtle was so impatient she wanted to just run across the road and hope for the best, but she was more sensible than that and just gritted her teeth and waited for the lollipop lady to waddle over to walk her across.

Once at the other side, Myrtle sprinted off again, down past the little park, round the church and up the narrow road that led past the allotments to her house. She was puffing and panting her way past the allotment gates when she saw something that made her stop in her tracks.

Out on the allotments, Mr McAndrew and another man were standing by the spot where the angel had crash-landed. The man with Mr McAndrew had a striped stick like an enormous ruler in his hand and was looking intently at the ground. Myrtle looked through the railings of the gate to get a better view and Mr McAndrew happened to look up and see her watching. He waved his arm to call her over. Myrtle shook her head but Mr McAndrew continued to wave her over and so she went through the gates and over to where they were standing.

"This is the young lady I was telling you about," Mr McAndrew said to the other man. "She lives in that house just over yonder. Keeps chickens in her garden, don't ye, Myrtle?"

Myrtle nodded. The other man smiled at Myrtle and shook her hand politely. He had extraordinarily long fingers, his eyes were small and shiny and he wore a crumpled suit and a spotty bow tie. Myrtle had never seen anyone real wearing a bow tie before.

"Hello, Myrtle," said the man. "I'm Professor Hoom."

"Hello," said Myrtle.

Now, Professor Hoom looked and acted like a perfectly polite and friendly person but there was something about him that Myrtle found a little, well, creepy. Maybe it was his extraordinarily long fingers or his shiny little eyes or maybe it was neither of those things. She couldn't explain it, even to herself, but a little voice inside her told her that underneath that polite and friendly manner, behind the jolly bow tie, Professor Hoom was not a person to be trusted.

"Professor Hoom has come about the meteor which fell right here," Mr McAndrew explained. "He's one of them scientist fellows. Knows about rocks and space and stuff."

"Meteor?" said Myrtle, pretending not to know anything.

"Observe," said Professor Hoom.

He stepped back and indicated the dip in the ground and the rows of squashed cabbages that the angel had landed upon.

"Something fell here last night," said Professor Hoom. "Came whizzing down from space and landed slap bang in the middle of these allotments and left this crater here. Did you happen to hear or see anything last night, Myrtle?"

"No," said Myrtle quickly.

"That's a shame. It would have been quite a spectacular sight. Could you hold this for me, please?"

Professor Hoom passed Myrtle his long, measuring stick.

"Just stand there with the stick, if you would."

Myrtle stood as she was asked. Professor Hoom pulled out a Polaroid camera that hung on a cord around his neck.

"I need to take a picture to show the size of the crater," he explained. "Smile!"

Professor Hoom pressed the shutter button and a grey picture rolled out of the front of the camera. Professor Hoom pulled the picture out by the edges and wafted it about to help the image develop.

"You've not yet asked where it is," said Professor Hoom.

"Pardon?" said Myrtle.

"The meteor. You haven't yet asked me where it is. And it plainly isn't here."

Professor Hoom looked her straight in the eye. His shiny little eyes fixing hers like headlights.

"I... I assumed you'd already taken it away," said Myrtle.

"No," said Professor Hoom. "But somebody did. Observe. There are footprints in the mud."

He pointed a long finger at a trail of footprints that could be clearly seen going away from the cabbage patch and towards the allotment gates.

"There are two sets of footprints. It looks like one of them was wearing trainers and the other wasn't wearing any shoes at all. They're not large footprints, are they?

The people who took it from here can't have been very big. Children, perhaps. You said you saw somebody skulking around the allotments last night, didn't you, Mr McAndrew?"

"That I did," said Mr McAndrew. "Didn't get a good look at them mind."

"Oh, I'm sure we'll find the thieves," said Professor Hoom. "And we'll get that lump of meteor too."

"What will you do with it when you get it?" asked Myrtle.

Professor Hoom smiled. It was a smile which made Myrtle uneasy.

"We'll take it away for tests," he said. "We'll cut it up and study what's inside it."

"Cut it up…?"

Myrtle mouthed the words to herself in horror, thoughts of what the scientist might do to her angel if he found him.

"I've got to go home now," said Myrtle, more desperate than ever to find the angel and make sure he was all right. She turned on her heel to walk away.

"Just wait a moment!" said Professor Hoom and slapped a hand on Myrtle's shoulder. Myrtle felt a shiver run down her spine.

"What is it?" she said.

"Observe," said Professor Hoom, holding out the developed Polaroid photograph of Myrtle standing with the measuring stick. "A perfect picture. You do have pretty smile, don't you? And we can even see the thieves' footprints, right there next to your own feet. Gosh, they're about the same size, aren't they?"

"I've got to go," said Myrtle and scurried away as fast as she could, out of the allotments, up the little road and through the gate into her own back garden. She bolted the gate shut and immediately felt a lot of better. After quickly checking on the chickens, Myrtle made her way up the garden to the garage, already thinking what she was going to tell the angel about what she had heard and learnt that day.

But Myrtle was in for a surprise. When she opened the door and stepped inside, she found the garage to be completely empty.

The angel had vanished.

7 – Bob

Distraught, Myrtle wracked her brain, trying to work out where the angel could possibly have gone. She searched every corner of the garage, poking around amongst the old paint tins, even lifting up the edge of the sleeping bag on the floor to look underneath. But, of course, the angel was not there.

Myrtle reluctantly left the garage and went into the kitchen where she found something most curious. An entire loaf of sliced white bread had been taken out of its bag and its contents scattered all over the kitchen work surface and floor. Some of the slices had been laid out neatly in rows on the surface, some pieces were stacked in piles, some lay on the floor and had quite clearly been trod upon. But, strangest of all, someone had stuffed six or seven pieces willy-nilly into the electric toaster and then tried to turn it on. Fortunately, the toaster wasn't plugged in or the resulting fire might have burnt down the whole house.

Myrtle stared and puzzled over the curious scene for a time. It simply made no sense. Myrtle called out for her mum.

"Mum! Are you in?"

There was no reply but there was a sudden bumping sound from upstairs as of something being dropped or knocked over.

"Mum?"

There was silence. Myrtle made her way from the kitchen, along the hallway and upstairs.

"Are you up here, Mum?"

Myrtle looked in her mum's bedroom, then Nanna's and then the bathroom but found no one. Finally, Myrtle went into her own bedroom and there, sat on the bed with a book in his hands, was the angel.

Myrtle didn't know whether to hug him or punch him.

"What are you doing up here?" she demanded. "You weren't in the garage. I thought something horrible had happened to you."

The angel gave her a sheepish little grin.

"I was bored," he explained. "There are so many exciting things to see and do in this world and I was stuck in that garage. I'm not complaining, Myrtle, but I just couldn't sit there all alone whilst there were so many things on Earth that I haven't experienced. So when I heard the two women leave the house a while ago -"

"You mean Mum and Nanna. They must have gone shopping."

"That's them. They left the back door open so I thought I would come inside for a bit. I've been reading some of your books. This one's great. It's about a boy, a prince, who lives on a little planet all by himself but for a flower and a sheep. It's fantastic."

"Look, I know," said Myrtle crossly. "I've read it ten times, maybe more. What is that mess in the kitchen downstairs? I assume you did that."

"Sorry," said the angel. "I was hungry too. I was trying to make toast but I couldn't get your toasting machine to work."

"You stuffed half a loaf of bread in it!"

"Oh," said the angel. "Was that wrong?"

"Yes!" Myrtle hissed.

"I'm sorry," said the angel and he did look genuinely apologetic. "There's a lot I don't understand. Things are so different here. But everything looks so fascinating." The angel stood up and went to the bedroom window which overlooked the road at the front of the house. "What's that there?" he said, pointing outside.

Myrtle looked.

"It's a car," she said.

"What's it do?"

Myrtle gave the angel a funny look.

"It takes people from place to place. Wherever they want to go."

"Wow! And what's that?"

"That? It's a TV aerial."

"What's it do?"

"You need one to get television."

"Television?"

Myrtle sighed.

"Television. You know, moving pictures which appear in a box."

"Amazing! And, oh look, here come those two women."

Myrtle looked down. Her mum and Nanna had rounded the street corner and were coming up towards the house. They were carrying six bulging carrier bags between them. Nanna puffed and panted as she wobbled along the pavement. Myrtle nearly screamed in panic.

"They're home!" she squealed. "Oh, no! They can't find you here! They can't!"

"What? Why? What's going on?" said the angel, unnerved by Myrtle's panic.

"No one must know you're here!" said Myrtle. "You must hide! Hide quickly!"

"Why must I hide?"

Myrtle's mind was suddenly filled with an image of the smiling but ever so slightly creepy Professor Hoom.

"Just have to," said Myrtle. "Quickly."

"Where?"

Myrtle considered hiding him under her bed but there were so many toys and games under there that there simply wasn't enough room for him. Instead, she pulled him over to her wardrobe and flung open the doors. Hanging clothes filled it from end to end.

"What has happened in here?" came a sudden cry from downstairs. "Myrtle! What have you been doing in this kitchen?"

Myrtle tried to push the angel into the wardrobe but he protested.

"It's too cramped," he said. "I'll never fit."

"Myrtle!" hollered Mrs Green. "Where are you?"

"There's nowhere else to hide you," Myrtle said to the angel.

"Then we'll have to think of something else," the angel replied.

Myrtle stared at the clothes hanging in the wardrobe.

"I've got an idea," she said. "You're about my size, aren't you?"

"I suppose so," said the angel.

Myrtle could hear her mum beginning to climb the stairs. She took a pair of jeans from the wardrobe.

"Put these on," she said.

The angel did as he was told, climbing into the jeans.

"Tuck your gown into the waist," said Myrtle and passed him a pair of trainers. "Slip these on."

"What are we doing?" said the angel, continuing to get dressed.

"Making a disguise," said Myrtle.

"But what about my wings?"

Myrtle pulled a thick duffel coat off its hanger.

"Try this," she said and helped the angel into the coat, careful not to press on his bandaged wing too much. The coat covered his wings well. He did look a little hunchbacked but that didn't matter.

Mrs Green's footsteps came pounding along the landing.

"What about my halo?" said the angel.

Myrtle bit her lip. No boy, wings or no wings, had a glowing light around his head. Her mum would spot that for sure.

Myrtle quickly grabbed an old striped bobble hat from the wardrobe's top shelf and rammed it over the angel's head just as her mum came barging into the room.

"Ah, so you are up here, young lady. That kitchen looks like an absolute bombsite!" snapped Mrs Green angrily and then abruptly changed her expression when she saw the angel stood next to Myrtle. "Oh, hello. Is this a friend of yours?"

The angel smiled sweetly at Mrs Green. The bobble hat, which came down all the way to the bottom of the angel's ears, managed to hide his glowing halo. Maybe the hat sparkled a little where light shone through but that was barely noticeable.

"Yes," said Myrtle. "This is a friend of mine from school."

"Oh, lovely," said Mrs Green to the angel. "She never brings friends home. And what's your name?"

The angel looked at Mrs Green and then at Myrtle. Myrtle stared at the angel and his sparkling bobble hat.

"Er, bobble… bobbie… Bob. Bob! His name's Bob, mum."

"Well, it's nice to meet you, Bob," said Mrs Green pleasantly. "Are you not too warm in that coat and hat?"

"No, I'm fine, thank you," said the angel. "I get cold easily."

"Well, Myrtle has to come downstairs now, Bob, and help tidy the kitchen before teatime. But do be sure to visit again."

"I will," said the angel.

Mrs Green gave the angel a cheerful grin and then, turning towards the door, gave Myrtle a brief but fiery stare that told her that she was still in trouble for the mess in the kitchen.

When Mrs Green was safely downstairs, Myrtle and the angel both breathed a heavy sigh of relief.

"That was close," said Myrtle.

The angel nodded in agreement.

"I like the name Bob though," he said.

Getting the angel back to the garage without arousing suspicion was a little difficult. Myrtle took the angel to the front door and told him to go out, walk round the corner and wait by the garden gate at the back of the house. Myrtle waved him off as he walked away, calling out loudly, "Goodbye, Bob. See you tomorrow."

Then, telling her mum that she had to go feed the chickens (which was true), Myrtle went down the garden and opened the gate to let the angel in. Finally, checking to see that no one was watching, Myrtle and the angel went back up towards the house and into the garage.

After tea, and after cleaning up the mess the angel had made in the kitchen, Myrtle snuck out to the garage with a bulging rucksack of things for the angel. In front of the angel's delighted eyes, Myrtle produced a packet of crisps, three chocolate biscuits, two apples and a handful of reading books.

"I'll enjoy reading these in bed tonight," said the angel, picking up the book he had been looking at earlier.

Myrtle was about to agree with him when she realised something.

"You won't be able to," she sighed. "I'm going to have to turn off the garage light otherwise mum will notice."

"That's okay," said the angel and whipped off his bobble hat, revealing his brightly shining halo once more.

And so, Myrtle said goodnight to the little angel and left him, reading a book by the light of his own halo.

8 - Chicks

The next day was a Saturday, so Myrtle did not have to get up so early and could have a little lie-in. But, as she lay dozing peacefully, she was awakened by her mum calling up to her.

"Myrtle! Myrtle! You've got a visitor!"

Myrtle rubbed her eyes, got up and plodded downstairs in her dressing gown. Mrs Green was stood by the open front door and on the doorstep, dressed in his hat and coat, was the angel. Myrtle blinked.

"It's me," said the angel. "Your friend Bob."

"Hello, Bob," said Myrtle coldly. "I didn't expect to see you here today."

"I thought I'd surprise you," he said.

"Yes, you did that. I have to get dressed."

"Come into the kitchen while you wait," Mrs Green said to the angel.

Myrtle trudged back upstairs to get dressed. She could hear her mum and the angel talking.

"Have you had any breakfast this morning, Bob?" Mrs Green was asking.

"No," said the angel.

"Would you like some?"

"Do you have toast?"

"Of course we do."

"Fantastic!" said the angel.

When she came downstairs again, Myrtle hurriedly went through to the kitchen, where the angel was sat at the breakfast table with Mrs Green and Nanna. The angel was happily munching into his third slice of toast.

"We're off to see the chickens," Myrtle told her mum and Nanna and hurriedly dragged the angel away from the table and out the back door.

"You shouldn't have done that," said Myrtle angrily as they walked down the garden.

"I was bored and hungry," said the angel. "This is a great disguise. Your family were really nice to me."

"Yes, but they won't be if they find out you're an angel."

The chickens were clucking loudly in their coop, eager to get out, to eat and to enjoy the sunshine. Myrtle nipped inside the run, unlocked the coop door and let the six noisy chickens out. They ran around Myrtle's legs as she prepared to put their food down. Belinda was jumping up and down in such excitement that Myrtle couldn't help but smile. When she put the food on the ground, the chickens huddled round the feeder and ate greedily.

"They were hungry too," said the angel.

"Help me collect the eggs," said Myrtle.

There was a little hatch in the back of the coop, which Myrtle could lift up to get the eggs the chickens had laid within. There were four eggs that morning. She gave two of them to the angel to hold.

"I didn't have time to tell you yesterday," said Myrtle, "but there's a man who's been looking for you."

"A man?" said the angel, frowning. "Who?"

"He's a scientist, Dr something-or-other. I met him on the allotments. He was measuring things. He told me he was looking for the thing that landed there the other night."

"What does he want with me?"

Myrtle shrugged. "He wants to take you away. To do tests on you." To cut you up, she added silently to herself. To cut you up and look at what's inside. "He knows there were two children on the allotments," she added. "I think he knows one of them was me."

"Oh, no!" said the angel.

"He might still be there today. Let's take a look."

Together, they went over to the fence at the bottom of the garden and peered through the gap between two slats. There were a half dozen early morning gardeners out on the allotments, including Mr McAndrew, but there was no sign of the scientist, Professor Hoom.

"Can't see him," said Myrtle.

"Hello," said a voice behind them.

Myrtle and the angel jumped in surprise and turned to face Professor Hoom who was stood right there in Myrtle's back garden. Myrtle was so surprised that she squashed together the two eggs she had been carrying, creating a gooey eggy mess in the palm of her hands.

"Sorry," said Professor Hoom. "I didn't mean to startle you."

Myrtle's heart pounded in her chest with fear.

"How did you get in?" she asked.

"The gate was open," said Professor Hoom, smiling. Myrtle decided that she really didn't like his smile. It made his tiny shiny eyes look even smaller.

"I must have left it open when I came round the house this morning," said the angel.

"You shouldn't just walk into someone's garden without asking," said Myrtle.

"No, you're quite right," said Professor Hoom, in a humble and apologetic voice, although Myrtle suspected he was just making fun of her. "But I thought you'd like to see this. Observe."

Professor Hoom held out what appeared to be a lump of bright white rock.

"It's a plaster cast," he said. "A model of one of the footprints that the thieves left on the allotment."

Myrtle could now see that plaster cast was exactly the same shape and size of her trainers.

"If we find the trainers that match this," said Professor Hoom, "then we will have found one of the thieves." He suddenly seemed to notice the angel. "You're new. Who are you?"

"I'm Bob," said the angel. "Are you Dr Something-Or-Other?"

"Professor Hoom. You're a friend of Myrtle's, right?"

"That's right."

"Fancy that. Well, I must be going. Work to do."

At that Professor Hoom walked back to the gate but turned to look at them one last time before going through.

"Nice pair of trainers you're wearing there, Bob," he smiled and then he was gone, closing the gate behind him.

Myrtle and the angel simply stood in silence for a while.

"He likes my trainers," said the angel.

"Those trainers are the ones I was wearing on the night I found you," explained Myrtle. "He knows. He knows everything about you and me. I can just tell."

Myrtle looked at her hands. They were coated with a horrible mixture of egg white, yolk and shell.

"Yuck!" she said and stuck out her tongue. "I'll have to wash this off."

"No, wait," said the angel and covered Myrtle's hands with his own.

"Don't. You'll get your hands dirty," said Myrtle but the angel ignored her.

The angel looked at their hands and seemed to concentrate his thoughts upon them. Myrtle began to feel a warm sensation, starting in the palms of her hands and spreading outwards. Then she noticed that the angel's hands had begun to glow with a light not unlike that of his halo.

"What are you doing?" asked Myrtle.

The angel removed his hands. The broken eggs that Myrtle had held were somehow, magically, whole again. It was as if the shells had been glued back together again and the runny innards shovelled back into them.

"How did you do that?" whispered Myrtle in wonderment.

"Healing hands," said the angel. "It's one of the angels' gifts. We're not just people with wings, you know."

"You're amazing."

The angel blushed. "Not finished yet. The eggs are still a little cracked."

He was right. There were some long wiggly cracks running around both eggs. The angel put his hands over Myrtle's again and concentrated. Myrtle felt the gentle warmth spread through her palms once more. It was a lovely, comforting feeling and she would have wanted it to go on forever but suddenly there was a cracking sound and something moved in her hand.

The angel felt it too and quickly removed his hands. Something truly remarkable had happened. Now, in Myrtle's hands, were two tiny yellow chicks. The fluffy little birds cheeped loudly and shook off the last bits of eggshell that clung to their feathers.

"Oh, my goodness!" said Myrtle.

"Oops," said the angel. "I think I've overdone it a bit."

"A bit?"

"Don't know my own strength sometimes."

Myrtle sighed deeply.

"We've got to find a way of getting you home soon," she said. "I don't think we can keep you a secret much longer."

The angel nodded.

"But what can we do?"

"We need to find out which star is your home," said Myrtle firmly. "We need to find out about the Celestial City. We need to find out everything we can about angels. We need information."

"And where will we get that from?"

"The library. There's one in the town."

"So you're off to the library then," said the angel.

45

"We're both going." Myrtle looked at the cheeping bundles of fluff in her hands. "Don't think I'm going to leave you here on your own."

9 – The Library

Myrtle made a nest of straw for the chicks in the corner of the coop. The six chickens took to them at once. Whilst a couple of the chickens ran to fetch mouthfuls of food for the chicks, Belinda clucked softly to them, like a mother singing a lullaby to her babies.

"I've never seen the chickens looking happier," said Myrtle. "Those chicks will be spoilt rotten. Come on, Bob. Let's go to town."

The angel was quivering with excitement as they walked down the road to the bus stop. He actually squealed with joy when the double-decker bus arrived at the stop and its doors hissed open. Myrtle paid for both of them and they went upstairs to sit by the windows at the front.

The angel loved the bus ride. He jiggled in his seat and pointed at every new thing that they passed.

"What's that?" he said.

"It's a traffic light," said Myrtle.

"What does it do?"

"It tells cars when to stop and when to go."

"What's that?"

"It's a playground."

"What's it do?"

"You play on it. You swing on the swings or slide down the slide."

"That looks amazing. Can we go there?"

"After the library," said Myrtle, sounding so very much like a parent talking to a child. "Library first, playground second."

"What's that?" said the angel, pointing again.

"It's a dog."

"Wow! What's it do?"

"Nothing. It's just a dog."

Myrtle was a little tired of the angel's unending questions but she also couldn't help being touched by the way in which everything seemed to cause him such delight. To the angel's eyes, the world was a thing of astonishing surprises, a constant wonder. The angel loved the world and everything in it and Myrtle couldn't remember ever having felt that way herself.

"This bus is fabulous," said the angel. "We're so high off the ground. It's just like flying."

Myrtle thought about the bandaged wing that the angel had hidden beneath his coat.

"Can't you use your healing hands to mend your wing like you did the eggs?" she asked.

"No," said the angel. "An angel's gifts are for helping others, not themselves. Hey, what's that?"

"That's the library. Our stop."

The angel waved at the bus driver when they got off and thanked him for the ride no less than three times.

"Now, we have to be quiet in here," Myrtle explained as they went through the library's big double doors.

"Why?" whispered the angel.

"Because we do," said Myrtle. "It's a rule. If you make a lot of noise, the librarians get angry and throw you out."

Myrtle went up to the information desk where a grey-haired lady in glasses was stamping dates in books.

"Excuse me," said Myrtle. "Can you help us find some books, please?"

"What were you looking for?" said the librarian.

"We wanted to find out where angels come from?"

"Where they come from?"

"Yes. A, er, friend of mine says that they come from this city, a long way away, which looks like a star from Earth. And I wanted to know which star it was."

The librarian looked deeply puzzled.

"Well," she said, "we might have some books about angels in the religion section, over there. But, if you wanted to find out about stars, you probably want to look in the science section. Some of the books have some lovely pictures of the different constellations."

"I think that's what we'll want," said Myrtle.

"Then the shelves you need are in that corner over there."

"Thanks," said Myrtle and guided the angel towards where the librarian had indicated.

"Look at all these books!" said the angel softly. "There are thousands of them! Are they all different?"

"Of course," said Myrtle.

"I never thought there could be so many books in the world."

"Well, we only want the ones that will help us get you home."

The science section had many, many books. Shelves full of them. Myrtle and the angel searched through the shelves, pulling out all the books that were about stars and outer space and putting them on a nearby table. Very soon they had a tall

49

and wobbly pile of books to look through.

Together, they sat down and began looking through them. As the angel sat marvelling at a picture of a purple and orange space cloud and Myrtle struggled to make sense of a diagram showing all the stars that could be seen from Earth, a boy took a chair near to them.

"I didn't know you were interested in astronomy," he said.

It was Isaac Adelman, Myrtle's classmate who had also seen the angel fall to Earth.

"Oh, hello," said Myrtle. "We were just looking. Browsing."

"I'm Bob," said the angel.

"Hi," said Isaac. "Why is your hat glowing?"

"Special wool," said Myrtle swiftly. "It's a new breed of sheep that has glowing wool."

"Oh," said Isaac, not entirely convinced. "These are great books, aren't they? I come here all the time to look at them. My Uncle David has bought me some books but they don't have pictures as wonderful as these. Look, that's the Horsehead Nebula. It's so beautiful."

"It is," agreed the angel.

"You understand this space stuff?" said Myrtle.

Isaac nodded enthusiastically.

"Oh, yes. I love it."

Myrtle pushed the book she had been looking at in front of Isaac.

"I don't understand any of this," she said.

"These are the constellations," Isaac explained. "That's Orion the hunter. That's Cygnus the swan. That one's the Southern Cross but you can't see that from here. You have to be in somewhere like Australia to see that."

Myrtle sighed to herself.

"This is all very complicated," she said. "Bob and I really wanted to learn about stars and where things were in space."

"Perhaps," said Isaac a little nervously, "you would like to... would you like to come over to my house? I could show you some things I've got. Space stuff."

"Could we?" asked the angel.

"That would be lovely," said Myrtle.

Isaac seemed surprised and relieved. "Really? You'd like that? Oh, that's great."

"But we have to go to the playground first," said the angel.

Myrtle glared at the angel.

"Isaac is going to help us," she said patiently. "We're going to his house."

The angel was sad.

"But you promised," he said. "Library first, playground second."

"He's just visiting," Myrtle said to Isaac. "They don't have playgrounds where he comes from."

"That's okay," said Isaac with a shrug. "I like the playground. We can go there."

"Hooray!" said the angel loudly, throwing his hands into the air.

At that moment a librarian came along and threw them out.

10 – The Playground

They walked to the playground, through the town centre and down by the riverside. All the while, the angel kept on pointing and asking questions.

"What's that?" he said.

"A zebra crossing," said Myrtle.

"What's it do?"

"Cars have to stop there if someone wants to cross."

"What, zebras?" said the angel.

"People," said Myrtle.

"What's that?"

"A fish and chip shop."

"Mmmm. Smells delicious. Even better than toast."

The angel gave a sudden gasp.

"The playground!" he yelled in delight. "We're here!"

With arms waving, the angel ran over to the brightly painted swings and slides. He was so giddy with excitement that he couldn't decide what to go on first but eventually chose the slide.

Isaac spoke to Myrtle as they walked briskly to catch up.

"Your friend's a bit strange, isn't he?" he said.

"What do you mean?" replied Myrtle.

"All these questions he keeps asking. It's like he's never been outside before."

"Well," said Myrtle slowly as she tried to think up a convincing explanation. "Bob's from a very remote island off the coast of… Wales. They don't have many of the things we do. They don't even have roads."

"But they do have sheep with glowing wool."

"Er, yes."

"I see," said Isaac thoughtfully. "Race you to the swings!"

Myrtle and Isaac sprinted for the swings. Myrtle just reached them first with Isaac hot on her heels. Laughing and panting they threw themselves back and forth on the swings. The angel meanwhile was climbing up and whizzing down the slide again and again, never seeming to tire of it and shrieking with utter joy every time he slid down.

Then the three of them went on the roundabout together, pushing it on to greater and greater speeds until the angel went quite pale and Myrtle felt she was going to throw up.

And after that, they all went on the seesaw, Myrtle and the angel on one side and the much larger Isaac on the other. Isaac was able to kick off from the ground with such force that Myrtle and the angel came crashing to the ground each time and were nearly shaken from their seat. The harder Isaac leapt, the more Myrtle and the angel laughed. The more they laughed, the harder Isaac leapt.

Exhausted by the roundabout and seesaw, the children flung themselves on the grass, stared up at the sky and looked for pretend shapes in the cotton wool clouds.

"That one looks like a dragon," said Myrtle.

"Nah. It's a wolf," said Isaac. "Now that one looks like an arm."

"Which one?"

"That one."

"That one there looks like a toaster," said the angel.

"Does not," giggled Myrtle.

"It does to me."

"That one looks like a train," said Isaac.

"It does, doesn't it?" said Myrtle.

"What's a train?" said the angel.

Isaac fixed the angel with a curious gaze.

"Don't they have trains where you come from, Bob?"

Behind the angel's back, Myrtle was giving the angel a manic look and shaking her head vigorously.

"Oh, trains," said the angel, catching Myrtle's frantic expression. "Er, yes, we have trains. Of course we do! We have trains all the time. Everywhere! Can't move for trains back home! I misheard you. I thought you said… brains."

"So you don't have brains where you come from then?"

"No," said the angel  cheerfully. "No brains. Not one. Gosh, never seen one of them."

Myrtle slapped her head into her hands. Isaac jumped to his feet and faced the girl and the angel.

"Okay, this isn't funny," he said firmly. "Are you two playing some kind of joke on me because it's not nice. I knew you were only pretending to be friends with me."

"That's not true," said Myrtle.

"You saw me in the library and said to yourself, 'Look, there's Isaac Adelman. He's got no friends and everyone picks on him so why don't we pick on him too.'"

"No," said Myrtle. "We wouldn't."

"Well, what is it then? Are you telling me that Bob really comes from a remote Welsh island where there's trains everywhere but no roads? Where apparently no one has a brain but, oh yes, you have whole flocks of luminous sheep. And that stupid hat. You've probably got a light bulb hidden in there or something."

Isaac bent down and, before either Myrtle or the angel could do anything, yanked the bobble hat off the angel's head. The piercing white light of the halo spilled out and shone all around.

11 – Angel's Song

Isaac staggered back, dumbfounded.

"What is that?" he said in breathless shock.

Myrtle looked around. Thankfully, there was no one else about in the park that day to see the angel's halo uncovered. She quickly snatched the bobble hat from Isaac and gave it back to the angel.

"It's his halo," she said quietly.

"What?"

The angel put his hat back on, hiding the light once more.

"My halo. I'm an angel."

Isaac simply stared.

"You won't tell anyone, will you?" pleaded Myrtle.

"Angels have wings," said Isaac.

"Under my coat," said the angel, tapping the bulge behind his shoulder. "I'm in disguise."

"You're an angel?"

The angel nodded.

"Called Bob?" said Isaac.

"It's not my real name."

"Please, please don't tell anyone," begged Myrtle. "It has to be a secret."

Isaac thought for a while. There was the rumble of distant thunder.

"The shooting star," said Isaac eventually. "That was you."

The angel nodded and Myrtle started to explain everything. While the white clouds above began to thicken and become grey and threatening, she told Isaac the whole story, about the shooting star and the allotments, about the damaged wing and the angel's powerful and wondrous name which could make you laugh and cry at the same time, about the Celestial City and the satellite, about Professor Hoom and the crushed eggs which became newborn chicks. She told him everything and he listened patiently until there was a surprisingly loud clap of thunder and it started to bucket down with rain.

There were no covered areas of the playground and no handy bus shelters nearby for them to hide in. However, there was a small church amongst the houses across the way and, at Myrtle's suggestion, they dashed towards it with their hands over their heads to protect themselves from the worst of the downpour.

The door to the church was open and they ran inside, shaking their arms to get rid of some of the water that had already soaked their coat sleeves.

"What horrible weather," commented an elderly man who was sweeping the floor between the pews. "Do come in. Don't be shy."

Dripping wet, they walked down the aisle to the seats at the front.

It was quite a lovely church. The wooden pews were a beautiful conker brown colour and smelled of polish. Comical stone gargoyles leered down at them from the ceiling. And, despite the grey weather outside, the church's stained glass windows were bright and colourful things, pictures of Bible stories, some Myrtle recognised and others she did not.

Myrtle sat down with a rain-soaked squelch. Isaac sat down next to her. "Never been inside a church before," he said.

"My parents used to take me to one when I was very young," said Myrtle. "Used to go to Sunday school too."

The angel went over to one of the stained glass windows. Steam was gently rising off his bobble hat.

The window contained a picture of a green hill beneath a dark blue sky. On the hillside stood three men amongst a group of white blobby sheep and hovering in the air above them were dozens of angels. Some of the angels were small and distant, little more than flashes of white. Others were larger but one in particular was as big as the shepherds on the hill and had his head down as though talking to them. He held a harp in his hand and spikes of white light, like lightning shot out from around his head.

"Angels. A whole company of them," whispered the little angel.

"It's when the angels came to tell the shepherds about Jesus' birth," explained Myrtle. "They're singing."

The angel smiled sadly.

"Yes. Songs so beautiful they'd make your insides ache," he said softly to himself. "We'd sing all day and all night if there were such things in the Celestial City. But it's daytime all the time because of the light created by my brothers' haloes." The angel reached out for but did not touch the stained glass window. "And the songs we'd sing. You have nothing like them. Can you imagine ten thousand voices singing in faultless harmony?"

And the angel began to sing, softly at first but then growing louder. It was a song without words. The angel's sweet little voice produced high clear notes, like the ringing of a bell or the vibrations of a crystal wineglass. The angel's voice rose up higher and higher and then dropped again, his melody turning this way and that.

It was, without any doubt or exaggeration, the most exquisite and touching sound that Myrtle had ever heard. Myrtle, Isaac and the man sweeping the floors all stopped and listened. It was music that made a person forget all their worries. It was music that reminded you, or almost reminded you, of something important that you had forgotten ages ago. The music was like the yellow light of dawn, like the sound of laughter, like the smell of freshly cut grass, like the feel of a warm blanket on a cold winter's night.

The music seemed to carry Myrtle up into the air as though she were as light as a leaf and, when the angel finally stopped singing, it took Myrtle a good few seconds to come to her senses once more.

The angel turned to Myrtle and Isaac. There were tears in his eyes.

"Angel songs. You have nothing like them."

Nobody spoke for a long moment after that and then Isaac said, "My Uncle David lives and works at an observatory by the seaside. He's an astronomer. They have the largest telescope in the country there. I go and visit him most Sundays. Perhaps you could come with me tomorrow. If anyone could find which star is your home, it's my Uncle David."

"You'll help me?" said the angel. "And you'll keep what I am a secret?"

Isaac nodded.

"I'll help you. It's the only good thing to do."

Myrtle couldn't contain her happiness. She gave Isaac a big soggy hug.

12 – A Trip to the Seaside

As soon as they were home, Myrtle asked her mum if it was okay for her to go visit Isaac's uncle the next day. Mrs Green readily agreed, pleased to hear that Myrtle had made two friends in as many days.

At nightfall, Myrtle and the angel went down to the chicken coop to put the birds to bed and to check on the chicks. The two little yellow birds were still happily hiding amongst the straw nest Myrtle had made for them, chirruping for the entire world to hear. Belinda had managed to dig up a worm for them and the chicks ate it greedily, gobbling at it from opposite ends.

Myrtle took some fruit and crisps from the house and brought them to the garage as a late supper for the angel. As the angel crunched into a juicy red apple, Myrtle looked at the bandaging on his wing. He told her it was feeling much better; not perfect, but better. Myrtle put a fresh bandage on and went back into the house to go to bed.

The next day, Sunday, Myrtle fed the chickens as usual and then got ready. At ten o'clock, an old battered car with big round headlights clattered to a stop outside the house. Isaac and his uncle got out. Isaac's uncle was a funny looking man. He had a long, serious face but his eyes were twinkly and mischievous. He came up to meet Myrtle and Mrs Green at the door of the house. He shook hands with both of them and introduced himself as Dr David Adelman.

"Are you sure you will cope with three children for the day?" asked Mrs Green.

"Indubitably, Mrs Green," he smiled. "I have enough boiled sweets to feed an army and more than a couple of tricks up my sleeve. But where is the third child?"

"Where's Bob?" Isaac asked Myrtle.

On cue, the angel came strolling round the corner of the street having walked up from the back gate of Myrtle's garden.

"There," said Myrtle.

"One, two, three. All accounted for," said Dr Adelman. "I shall bring yours back before midnight, Mrs Green, intact and unharmed."

Dr Adelman bundled the three youngsters into the back seat of the car, started up the rattling engine and, with a wave out of the window for Myrtle's mum, drove off down the road towards the coast.

On the way they played I Spy and Animal, Vegetable or Mineral. They sang songs, counted cars and told jokes. In what seemed no time at all, they saw the sea, a grey-blue strip between sky and ground, and not too many minutes after that they were driving along the seafront, with rows of tall and gaily painted hotels on one side and the beach and sea upon the other.

It was not a particularly warm day and there were no holidaymakers in the town. Many of the amusements and attractions were closed. Nonetheless, the children wanted to get out, explore and play. It had been years since Myrtle had been to the seaside and, of course, the angel had never been at all.

Dr Adelman took them onto the pier where he gave each of them a small amount of money to spend. Isaac and Myrtle immediately bought ice creams with chocolate flakes in them. The angel bought himself a big bag of candyfloss, half of which he managed to get stuck to his face.

There were some fairground rides on the pier, a few of which were running, and so together Myrtle, Isaac, the angel *and* Dr Adelman went on the dodgem cars, racing around the floor and knocking each other silly when they collided.

Giggling and stumbling, they went down to the end of the pier to look at the sea. The breeze off the sea pinched at their cheeks and filled their noses with the sea's salt smell. Seagulls circled overhead, opening their sharp beaks to caw hungrily at the three people and the angel below.

Myrtle found a chip that someone had dropped on the pier and threw it up to the gulls. The gulls dived for it and one of them, the fastest, managed to snatch the chip out of the air and carry it away with his fellow gulls in hot pursuit.

From the pier, the four of them went down onto the beach. It was far too cold to go paddling but they stood at the water's edge and threw pebbles into the waves as they rolled in. When they had tired of that, Dr Adelman took them back up the beach to his car.

"Right," he said, "put your hand up if you own the largest telescope in the country."

Myrtle, Isaac and the angel watched as Dr Adelman slowly raised his own hand.

"Oh. That's right. It's me," he said, pretending to be surprised. "Now, who wants to go see it?"

The children jumped up and down cheering and, in moments, they were all back in the car, driving off to visit Dr Adelman's observatory.

13 – The Observatory

They drove a little way along the seafront, away from the town, until the coastline became rugged and the winding road led them along high cliffs. Dr Adelman's observatory stood upon the edge of one of the cliffs. It was a strange looking building and sort of put Myrtle in mind of a windmill that had lost its sails. The observatory building was tall, white and perfectly round. The top of the observatory was a large dome.

"The telescope's in that dome," said Isaac as they came near.

Dr Adelman parked up and they all piled out.

"Welcome! Welcome all!" cried Dr Adelman loudly with his arms outstretched, as though he were a ringmaster introducing an amazing circus act, and then he skipped, actually skipped over to the observatory and opened the door for them to go inside.

"Your uncle's a bit weird, isn't he?" Myrtle whispered to Isaac.

"A bit," said Isaac.

"I think he's great," said the angel.

The ground floor rooms of the observatory were where Dr Adelman lived. There was a kitchen and dining room, a bedroom and a tiny little bathroom. Dr Adelman quickly led them through his living quarters and then up a spiral staircase to his work rooms above.

There was a room full of computers and charts and piles of books and papers. It was an untidy mess of a room but Dr Adelman either didn't notice or didn't care.

"This is where all the boring stuff goes on," he explained. "This is where I record all my findings. As the old astronomy saying goes, if it isn't written down, it didn't happen."

"Is that true?" asked the angel.

Dr Adelman grinned.

"You tell me, Bob," he said.

"What things do you write down?"

"I write down everything I see through the telescope. Maybe I will spot something new. A star or a comet. If I do, I'll make a note of where I saw it and then it's given a name so that other people will know what to call it when they see it in their telescopes."

The angel nodded thoughtfully.

"Why?" he asked.

"Why?" said Dr Adelman. "Because that's what we do. We measure, we record and we add to the growing number of things that are known about our universe."

"And does that make you happy?"

The question seemed to flummox Dr Adelman. He just looked at the angel with his half-smile still stuck on his face.

In the end he said, "Let's go look at the telescope, eh?"

They climbed another spiral staircase and came up through a trapdoor into a huge room with a ceiling that was curved and round like the inside of a ball but as high as a house. They were inside the dome on top of the building. And even though the room was huge it was almost filled by the fat, shiny tube of Dr Adelman's telescope. Myrtle had no idea it would be so large. She had imagined it would be something that would be large but small enough for a person to carry from place to place, but this monstrously huge thing would take a crane to lift and a lorry to transport.

"Flaming Nora!" said Myrtle. "It's as big as a car!"

"Actually, it's longer than three cars put end to end," said Dr Adelman. "And the lens at the end is as tall as a man. Come and see."

The telescope was pointed up at an angle, its weight held up by thick steel girders and they had to climb a small set of steps in order to see the circular glass lens on its upward pointing end. It was, as Dr Adelman had said, as tall as a man and the cleanest piece of glass Myrtle had ever seen.

66

"Please do not touch it," said Dr Adelman. "The lens has to be perfectly flat and clean if I am to get accurate measurements."

The angel was staring at the curved wall opposite the lens.

"But how can it see the stars if there's a wall in the way?" he asked.

"Ah-ha!" exclaimed Dr Adelman. "That's the fun bit. Isaac, would you go press the button for us?"

Isaac scrambled down the steps and across to a panel of switches and buttons on the wall. In the middle of the panel was a big red button and Isaac pushed this.

A loud mechanical groaning started up which seemed to come from all around them and a most astonishing thing happened. A crack appeared in the high ceiling of the observatory, letting in a thin, bright line of daylight. Startled, Myrtle and the angel drew closer together.

"Don't worry," laughed Dr Adelman. "Watch."

The crack above them slowly grew wider and wider and Myrtle saw that the curved walls and ceiling of the observatory were rolling aside, like two halves of an Easter egg being taken apart. When the clanking and groaning eventually stopped, there was a thick gap running right across the room through which the telescopes lens could clearly see. A cool sea breeze came in through the gap and wafted over them.

"Clever, isn't it?" said Dr Adelman.

"Not half," said Myrtle, gobsmacked. "It's like having a sunroof on your house."

"Can we have a look

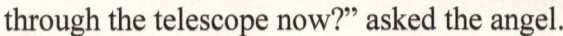

through the telescope now?" asked the angel.

67

"Well, we won't be able to use it right now, I'm afraid," replied Dr Adelman. "We have to wait until it gets dark."

"Aw," sighed Myrtle disappointed. "But that's hours away."

"Time enough to get ready for dinner. I need some helpers in the kitchen and you are not my only dinner guests this evening. We have another guest coming along the later."

"Who is it?" asked Isaac.

Dr Adelman tapped the side of his nose.

"Well, that's a secret that will have to keep. Come on then, everyone. Downstairs now. We have lots to do."

So, downstairs they went and into Dr Adelman's kitchen where they all cheerfully mucked in with the preparations for dinner. Myrtle and Isaac peeled potatoes and the angel shelled peas into a bowl. Then, as Dr Adelman put on his apron and set about cooking sausage, mash and peas, the children mixed jelly cubes and hot water together to make five large bowls of strawberry jelly and then laid out the tablecloth, the plates, the glasses, the knives, forks and spoons. It was as Dr Adelman was draining the potatoes ready for mashing that there came a rat-a-tat knock on the door.

"That will be our dinner guest," said Dr Adelman, giving the pan of potatoes a good shake. "Let him in, would you?"

Isaac, Myrtle and the angel went to the door together and opened it. Myrtle gasped in horror. On the doorstep stood Dr Adelman's dinner guest, dressed in a crumpled suit and a spotty bow tie.

It was Professor Hoom.

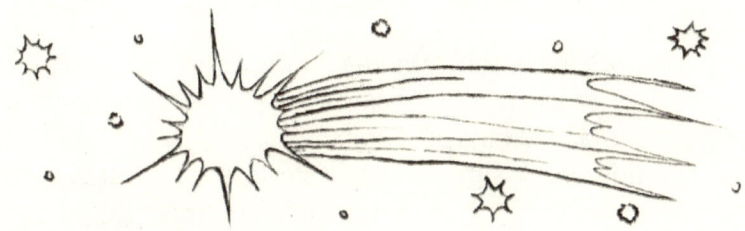

14 - The Unexpected Dinner Guest

Myrtle and the angel were truly struck dumb with a mix of shock and terror but Isaac, who had never met the professor before, welcomed him politely.

"Do come in," he said in a very grown up voice. "May I take your coat?"

"Why thank you," said Professor Hoom, stepping inside. "And good evening to you, young people. Why, it's Myrtle, isn't it? And Bob, the boy with the dashing trainers. Fancy meeting you here."

Myrtle and the angel managed to utter the faintest of hellos.

"Is that dinner I smell?" said Professor Hoom, sniffing. "It smells delicious."

"This way," said Isaac and led Professor Hoom through to the kitchen. The angel and Myrtle exchanged worried looks and followed them.

When Professor Hoom entered the kitchen, Dr Adelman put down the big bowl of mashed potatoes he was carrying and shook Professor Hoom's hand with great enthusiasm.

"Professor, so glad you could make it. And right on time too. Sit down everyone. Let's tuck in."

The five of them squeezed in around the small table. Myrtle made sure that the angel was sat as far away from Professor Hoom as possible. Dr Adelman frowned at the angel.

"Do you intend to wear that coat and woolly hat at the dinner table, Bob?" he asked.

"Yes. I never take them off," said the angel quickly. "I get cold easily."

Dr Adelman said nothing more of it and served up large helpings of potatoes and sausages. As he offered around the bowl of peas he made the introductions.

"Children, this gentleman is Professor Hoom. He and I have been friends for many years although we do not get to meet up as often as I would wish. Like me, he is an astronomer and has forgotten more about outer space than I have ever learnt. Professor, this is my nephew, Isaac. He is a keen stargazer too, aren't you, Isaac? And these are two of Isaac's school chums, Myrtle and Bob."

"Yes," said Professor Hoom. "We've already met. I had the pleasure of talking to these two youngsters only yesterday. Myrtle's house backs onto the allotments where that meteor crashed the other night."

"How exciting is that?" said Dr Adelman. "Isaac here actually watched it fall to earth through his telescope. Isn't that right, Isaac?"

Isaac was unable to answer as he had a mouth full of sausage.

"Well, what an amazing coincidence," said Professor Hoom, his small eyes fixing on each child in turn. "One friend sees the meteor land almost in the other friend's back yard. Since I have still not managed to locate the fallen meteor, it's probable that these young people know more about this particular incident than any other person in the entire world. I must pick their brains later."

The angel gasped in horror and clutched Myrtle's hand under the table.

"Are you all right, Bob?" asked Professor Hoom, giving the angel one of his creepy smiles.

"He's fine," said Myrtle.

"The sausages are a little hot," said the angel. "I burnt my tongue. Bit surprised, that's all."

Satisfied, Professor Hoom tucked into his dinner and began to talk to Dr Adelman about people the children did not know, places they'd never been and something called a 'university'. But, every so often, his eyes would wander to Myrtle and the angel, never letting them far from his sight.

"Are you okay?" Myrtle whispered to the angel at a moment when Professor Hoom was not looking at them.

The angel looked like he was about to cry.

"He said he was going to pick out your brains," he replied. "It sounds awful."

"Pick our brains," said Myrtle. "Not pick *out* our brains. He just means he wants to ask us some questions. Though that's bad enough."

The dinner was very tasty indeed but Myrtle and the angel were too nervous and fearful to enjoy it at all. When everyone had finished, the children helped to tidy the plates away and served up the bowls of strawberry jelly they had made earlier.

"Not for me," said Professor Hoom. "Jelly's far too slimy. Can't stand the stuff."

"All the more for us then," said Dr Adelman and waggled his eyebrows at the children.

As the others ate their jelly, Professor Hoom took an apple for himself from the fruit bowl on the table and began to peel it with his knife.

"So, doctor, have you shown the youngsters your telescope yet?"

"We were going to have a look after dinner," said Dr Adelman. "It will be dark soon and a fine clear night for looking at the stars."

"We're very excited," said the angel.

"Of course you are," said Professor Hoom. "Perhaps hoping to get a glimpse of a little green man from Mars." He laughed to show that he was joking.

"I'd love to meet a person from another planet," said Isaac. "A real alien."

"Would you? Would you really?" said Professor Hoom.

"Oh, yes. I'd meet him as he got out of his little spaceship and say, 'Hello. Welcome to Earth.'"

"Wouldn't you be scared?"

Isaac shrugged. "I kind of guessed it would be a friendly alien."

"But how would you know?" said Professor Hoom, cutting a slice of apple and holding it out on the end of his knife. "Observe. If a stranger, someone you did not know at all, offered you a piece of apple, would you take it?"

Isaac raised his hand as if to take the slice of apple from Professor Hoom but hesitated.

"No," he said. "I don't take things from strangers."

"Even if they look friendly and harmless?"

"Not even then," said Isaac.

"Well said," nodded Dr Adelman.

"It's the same with things from outer space," said Professor Hoom pointing up with his knife as though pointing out the stars in the sky. "It's a wild and dangerous universe out there. Anything that lands on Earth must be regarded with the utmost suspicion. It could be poisonous or radioactive or sent with some wickedness in mind."

Myrtle couldn't be sure but he appeared to be looking directly at the angel as he said this.

"If someone or something from up there were to land near my home, I would assume it was dangerous until it had been proven otherwise," the Professor went on.

"And how can you prove something isn't dangerous?" asked the angel.

"Tests," said Professor Hoom. "Experiments and examination by the proper authorities. For example, if I had been the first person to find whatever it was that fell into those allotments I would have called the police or something. For my own safety, you understand. Who knows what dangers it possesses."

"And if it were dangerous," said the angel, "what would they do with it?"

"The authorities? They would lock it away or, if they thought it to be a serious threat, they would destroy it."

The angel squeezed Myrtle's hand so hard that Myrtle yelped. Everyone stared at her.

72

"Sorry. I stubbed my toe on the table leg," she said and hurriedly finished her jelly.

With dinner done, Isaac suggested that he and Myrtle and the angel help clear away the dinner plates but Dr Adelman said no.

"You three run along upstairs. Go see if it's dark yet. Professor Hoom and I will tidy up down here and join you shortly."

And so, the three friends climbed up the spiral staircases, first to the room full of computers and then higher still to the huge domed room with the telescope in. Night had fallen and through the gap in the dome they could see a clear, starry sky.

But the poor angel was not able to enjoy the beautiful view. He was shaking with panic and would not let go of Myrtle's hand.

"Did you hear what he said?" the angel cried. "He thinks I'm dangerous. He wants to lock me up. Throw away the key, he will. Or worse..."

"He doesn't know it was you who fell into the allotments," said Isaac.

"Oh, he does," said the angel. "He knows. I can just tell."

Myrtle patted the angel's shoulder but could say nothing to comfort him. She was sure that the angel was right. Professor Hoom knew. Somehow he knew and very soon he would be coming up those stairs and Myrtle did not know if she had the courage to face him again.

15 – Escape from Professor Hoom

"You're worrying about nothing," said Isaac. "Professor Hoom still thinks it was a meteor that fell to Earth that night and, Myrtle, I doubt he really suspects you found it – I mean him."

"But it's the way he looks at me," said Myrtle.

"It's like he can see into your heart," said the angel.

"See what you're thinking."

"Piffle," said Isaac. "He's got a funny stare. So what? He knows nothing and he won't know anything unless one of you two does something silly."

Myrtle and the angel were not convinced.

"I bet he's phoning the police right now," said Myrtle. "Or maybe he phoned them before he even arrived and they've got the place surrounded at this very minute."

"Now you're being silly," sighed Isaac. "I tell you what, let's go downstairs quietly and have a listen and then we'll see if he's phoning the police or not."

So, the children crept down the spiral stairs, down the first set of stairs to the computer room and then halfway down the second set to where they could hear Professor Hoom and Dr Adelman still talking in the kitchen. The children and the angel huddled together on the steps and listened.

"How can you be sure?" Dr Adelman was saying.

"Because I can smell a lie a mile away," replied Professor Hoom. "That girl, Myrtle, is hiding something and that Bob… There's something very peculiar about him."

"That proves nothing."

"True. But I have a plaster cast of one of the thieves' footprints and I am willing to bet my life that it matches Bob's trainers."

"So what are you going to do?"

"I'm going to go up there now and confront them with the truth."

"And if they don't own up?" asked Dr Adelman.

"Then I am quite prepared to get the police involved. I'm sure a thorough search of the children's homes and belongings will turn up something."

On the dark stairs, the children listened in shock.

"You were right," Isaac whispered to Myrtle. "What shall we do?"

"We have to get away," said Myrtle. "If they search Bob here, they're bound to notice his wings and then…"

She said nothing more. She did not want to think about what the likes of Professor Hoom would do if they discovered the truth about the angel.

There was the sound of the kitchen door being opened and of footsteps coming towards the stairs.

"He's coming," said Myrtle. "Upstairs. Quickly!"

The three of them dashed up the stairs. There was nowhere to run to or hide in the computer room so they carried on up to the top but once there they realised it was a dead end.

"There's no way out," exclaimed Myrtle.

The angel ran to the gap in the dome. There was a short wall running across the gap to stop people accidentally falling out of the dome and down to the ground. The angel climbed onto the little wall and looked down the outside of the observatory building.

"We could jump down."

"Don't," said Isaac. "You'd break your legs and that's if you were lucky enough to not jump right over the cliff. We're right next to it and the sea is a long way down."

"A very long way down," said a voice behind them.

Professor Hoom had appeared at the top of the stairs without the children noticing. Dr Adelman was stood on the steps behind him.

"You've got nowhere to run to," said the professor and reached out to grab hold of Myrtle's arm. Myrtle shrieked, twisted away from his long fingers and ran over to the angel.

"Don't do anything silly," said Dr Adelman to Myrtle. Or maybe he was talking to Professor Hoom. It was hard to tell. Professor Hoom walked slowly towards Myrtle. Myrtle climbed onto the wall next to the angel to be further away from him.

"Don't!" cried out Dr Adelman. "It's not safe. Professor, please stay back."

The wind whistled around Myrtle's body, tossing her hair around and making her legs tremble. She could sense but not see the long drop behind her. She was scared to think about how far down the ground really was.

"Please get down, children. No one's angry with you. No one's in any trouble," said Dr Adelman, trying to sound calm and friendly.

"Oh, but they are in trouble," said Professor Hoom in a far less pleasant voice. "You're a couple of light-fingered thieves, aren't you? Admit it."

Myrtle spread her arms in front of the angel to protect him.

"Stay back!" she shouted. "You can't have him!"

Professor Hoom laughed.

"There's nowhere to go. You won't jump," said Professor Hoom. "You're not quite that stupid."

"Please," begged Dr Adelman. "Just come down."

"You don't have any other choice," said Professor Hoom.

The angel undid his thick duffel coat and slipped it off. The wind caught it and blew it up high into the air.

"What are you doing?" Myrtle said to him.

The angel did not reply. He reached over his shoulder and ripped the bandage from his wing. As his glossy white wings unfurled, Professor Hoom, Dr Adelman and little Isaac stared in wonder.

"What is going on?" gasped Professor Hoom. "Those are…"

"His wings," said Isaac.

Myrtle looked at the angel.

"You hurt your wing. You said you wouldn't be able to fly."

"It feels a lot better now," said the angel and with that he wrapped his arms around Myrtle's waist and jumped backwards into the air, dragging Myrtle with him.

16 – Flying

In the darkness, Myrtle fell, tumbling end over end, the wind roaring in her ears. She did not scream but she closed her eyes and waited for the cold, hard earth to come up and hit her as she knew it would.

But it never did.

After a long time of falling without hitting anything, Myrtle opened one eye and saw the sea passing by directly below her. The gentle waves were less than an arm's length beneath her.

The angel was above her, still holding her firmly in his arms. His wings – and they were even more beautiful in the moonlight – were spread wide, slowly and softly flapping up and down like those of a soaring eagle. They were flying!

"Am I dreaming?" asked Myrtle. "Or am I dead?"

The angel laughed.

"As far from either as it's possible to be."

Myrtle couldn't resist reaching down and letting her fingers splash through the tops of the waves. The water was icy cold but Myrtle didn't care.

They flew on and Myrtle saw they were heading towards the multicoloured lights and illuminations of the seaside town.

"Won't people see us?" she said.

"Does it matter anymore?" the angel replied.

The angel took them high up, making Myrtle's stomach sink, and flew in over the pier. Many of the people walking on the pier did not notice the angel and the girl up high in the sky but those that did stopped and stared. One little boy dropped his candyfloss and shouted, "Look, mum! It's a fairy!" But by the time the boy's mother had looked up, Myrtle and the angel had passed them by and were flying in towards the town.

The town was an amazing thing to see from the air. Myrtle could see how all the buildings large and small bunched together, some in neat rows, others in higgledy-piggledy lines. She saw the secret rooftops and terraces that no one on the ground knew about. She saw the gargoyles, inscriptions and carvings on tall old buildings that no one paid attention to anymore. She saw how the streetlights formed connecting chains across the town and wondered if anyone really understood what a beautiful thing the people of the town had built for themselves.

The angel flew on and, in time, they left the town and were gliding out over moonlit countryside.

"Where are we going?" asked Myrtle.

"I'm taking you home," said the angel.

He apparently knew where he was going. He flew on in a straight line, never once stopping or changing direction. They occasionally crossed roads and followed one for a while. They even flew alongside a railway line for a time, the angel racing against a commuter train as it sped its passengers homewards.

Myrtle decided that flying was the most fantastic thing ever. The angel carried her high, swooped down low with her. He could twist and turn with the slightest tilt of his wings. The wind seemed to love him and to carry up him as a parent would carry a child on their shoulders.

Myrtle could only imagine what it must have been like for the angel being unable to fly. It must have been like losing one's arms or legs. No. Worse. It must have been like losing the ability to laugh or smile or show any kind of joy. Myrtle's love for the angel was boundless and now, sharing the magic of flight with him, her resolve to help him get home was all the stronger.

Soon enough though, their journey came to an end. The fields and woodlands they were gliding over gave way to houses and little streets and Myrtle saw that they were now flying above her home town. There were the shops that Myrtle knew so well. There was the park and the church in which they had sheltered from the rain. Myrtle even managed to spot where her school was though it was dark and lightless. And there, she noticed, the allotments and her own back garden.

The angel slowed and gently brought them down into the garden. Myrtle's feet touched down upon the grass and she stumbled, wobbling, away from the angel.

Myrtle laughed and spun around on tiptoes.

"That was incredible," she said, giving the angel a hug. "You're incredible."

The angel smiled, blushing a little.

"Thank you," he said.

"And you can fly again," said Myrtle. "You'll be able to fly home."

"Only if I know where I'm going," the angel replied. "I still don't know which star is my home."

"Of course. I forgot about th-"

Myrtle stopped.

She was looking at the chicken coop and had seen something that made her blood run cold.

A big hole had been dug underneath the wire fence of the chicken run, a hole made by some large burrowing animal.

"Oh, no," Myrtle moaned softly and rushed over to the run to look inside.

There were feathers lying around everywhere. There was no sign of the chickens.

17 – The Fox

Myrtle went into the chicken run and then into the coop itself. Her heart lifted momentarily when she saw five petrified chickens and two little chicks huddled together in the corner of the coop but when she realised that there were only five chickens and no more than that, the feelings of dread and horror returned. Belinda, Myrtle's favourite chicken and until recently her only friend, was missing.

Myrtle came out of the coop.

"Belinda's gone," she told the angel, holding back her tears of anguish. "A fox must have got her."

"There's a hole in the fence here," said the angel, pointing out the, broken fence slats and the gaping hole that had not been there that morning. "That's how he must have got through. Let's look."

"No," said Myrtle. "You must fly. Get away."

The angel shook his head. "Not yet. There are more important things than me."

Though it seemed pointless to try to find Belinda, Myrtle clambered through the hole in the fence to see what lay beyond. She came through into the allotments.

"There are tracks here," she said, "but I can't see them very well."

The angel squeezed through the hole to stand beside her. He took his bobble hat off and his halo light shone upon the ground.

"Now can you see?" he said.

Myrtle could make out a set of tracks in the mud, leading off towards the potting sheds.

"This way," she said and they followed the tracks as quickly as they could.

Myrtle was desperate to see where the tracks led but also fearful of what she would find at the end. What she did not expect to find was Mr McAndrew but find him she did, standing quiet and alone with his torch turned off by his side. Scurrying after the trail of fox prints, Myrtle and the angel came upon him quite suddenly but he did not seem at all surprised to see them.

"Ach, it's you two, is it?" he said.

Myrtle thought there was no sensible answer to that so she said nothing. She then realised that Mr McAndrew was looking down at something on the ground and Myrtle saw that it was Belinda. The chicken lay perfectly still in the mud, her white feathers ruffled and matted with dirt.

"I saw a fox running across the way with her in his mouth," said Mr McAndrew quietly. "I chased the fox away but..." He sighed. "I'm sorry, Myrtle."

Myrtle could contain her sadness no longer. The tears flooded from her eyes and she sobbed as she had never sobbed before. Mr McAndrew took her in his arms and hugged her to his side. Myrtle pressed her face into his shirt, dampening it with her tears.

Meanwhile, the little angel had crouched down by the chicken and carefully scooped her body up in his hands.

"This is wrong," he said.

Mr McAndrew shrugged and said not unkindly, "Foxes have to eat. If it isn't chicken, it's something else."

"But this was Myrtle's friend," said the angel. "And Myrtle is my friend."

Sniffing noisily, Myrtle looked as the angel enfolded the chicken in his arms.

The angel's hands began to glow, softly at first but with slowly increasing brightness.

The angel stared fiercely at the chicken as he concentrated upon her lifeless body. The light and warmth that flowed from his hands grew and grew until Belinda was lost in the glare. And the angel's halo too grew in brightness, from mere torchlight to a dazzling starlight shine.

The angel's stare deepened as he worked his magic upon the chicken. Myrtle and Mr McAndrew had to step back and shield their eyes, such was the power of the angel's light. Brighter and brighter it shone, moment upon moment, until it was as if the sun itself was standing in the allotments.

And then, in an instant, the angel's light went out and Myrtle and Mr McAndrew found themselves in sudden and complete darkness.

"What's happened? What's happened?" called out Myrtle, feeling around in the darkness.

"Here," said the angel's voice faintly and something soft and warm was placed in Myrtle's hands. At first, she couldn't work out what it was but then the soft and warm thing clucked and Myrtle knew.

"Belinda!" she cried and the chicken wriggled happily against Myrtle's chest.

"Well, I'll be darned," said Mr McAndrew. "She's been made as good as new."

"Just about," said the angel. The light of his halo had returned to normal – perhaps it was even weaker than before – and, by that light, Myrtle could see that the angel was looking pale and exhausted.

"Are you all right?" she asked.

The angel tried a smile but he was too tired.

"Mending eggs is easy but whole chickens is harder," he said weakly. "I am only a little angel after all."

"You look absolutely jiggered. We'd better get you sat down before you fall down," said Mr McAndrew. "Let's get you to me shed and I'll put a brew on."

Mr McAndrew slipped his hand under the angel's arm to support him and the four of them, the old man, the angel, the girl and the chicken, made their way over to the potting sheds.

18 – Mr McAndrew's Potting Shed

Mr McAndrew's potting shed was small, cramped but curiously inviting. One wall was lined with tools and shelves packed closely with seeds and pots and odds and ends. But the rest of the shed was given over to creature comforts. There was a tatty and threadbare armchair and a small table and upon the table sat an electric kettle, some mugs, a portable radio and a small lamp. The place was like a tiny little living room. There was even a picture hanging on the wall and curtains over the window.

Mr McAndrew helped the angel in and carefully set him down in the armchair.

"Right. Who's for some nettle tea?" he said and turned on the kettle.

Myrtle set Belinda down on the floor. Something had been bothering her for several minutes and now she felt she had to say something.

"Excuse me, Mr McAndrew," she said, waving her hand towards the angel. "Doesn't this seem a little odd to you?"

"Well, I admit nettle tea is an acquired taste but the only other thing I've got is some of last year's rhubarb wine and I think you're too young for that."

"That's not what I meant. Doesn't anything about Bob's appearance strike you as a little strange?"

Mr McAndrew stroked his scraggly beard thoughtfully.

"Apart from him being an angel, you mean? Not really," he said and, as the kettle clicked off, poured out three mugs of a dark, hot liquid.

"You don't seem too bothered about him being an angel," Myrtle said, taking a mug of the nettle tea from Mr McAndrew.

"Don't see why I should be. Fact is, he's clearly an angel. Always believed in them since I was a lad so I shouldn't be surprised if I see one. Actually thought I did see one once, when I was just a wee child."

"Really?"

"Aye. One night, I was looking down from my bedroom window and I saw something moving in the neighbour's yard. It was a man or something like a man and he had something on his back. Couldn't quite see it but it was all sparkling in the moonlight. Thought it was his angel wings, you see. So I pelted downstairs, out the back door and all but leapt over the fence into next-door's."

"And?" said Myrtle.

"It wasn't an angel. It was a burglar. Had an open sack of next-door's silver on his back. He'd just stolen it. Of course, I gave him the fright of his life, running up to him like that. He dropped the sack and fled."

Mr McAndrew sighed heavily.

"And now, years later, I finally get to meet a real angel." He looked at the tired little angel in the armchair. "Mind you, I expected him to be taller. Anyway, drink up now."

Myrtle and the angel sipped at their nettle tea cautiously.

"Good, isn't it?" said Mr McAndrew.

Myrtle thought it tasted like old socks and grass cuttings and she could tell by the angel's expression that he disliked it just as much. But the angel drank it down bravely and said, "It's delicious. Really nice."

Mr McAndrew smiled proudly.

"Thank you. My own special blend that is. So does anyone else know about our angelic friend here?"

"His name's Bob," said Myrtle, "and, yes, some people do know. My friend, Isaac, Isaac's uncle and Professor Hoom."

"Hoom? That scientist with the beady eyes and fingers like spider legs?"

"Professor Hoom wants to take Bob away and lock him up," said Myrtle. "All he wants is to do tests and experiments on him."

"Well, some people are like that," said Mr McAndrew. "I just accept things as they are but others always need to know how something works or why it is there. Scientists are the worst for that. Professor Hoom thinks that Bob is something strange and mysterious. And things he doesn't understand make him afraid. So, he wants to do one of two things. Either poke and prod at Bob until he does understand or get rid of Bob altogether."

"But that's so cruel," said Myrtle angrily.

"But only because he's scared. It's just the way he is. I suppose we should pity him for that, not hate him."

Mr McAndrew peered out of the window through the gap in the curtains.

"And do you reckon this Hoom fellow might have called the police?"

"Perhaps," said Myrtle. "Why?"

"Because they're here," Mr McAndrew replied. "Look."

"Already?" said Myrtle, despairingly. "I thought we'd have longer than this!"

She looked through the curtains. There were several figures out on the allotments. Each of them was carrying a torch, waving it this way and that. And further away, beyond the allotment gates, some police cars were parked, their blue emergency lights flashing on and off.

"Reckon they've got us pretty much surrounded," said Mr McAndrew. "Have you got enough energy to fly away, Bob?"

The angel shook his head.

"I'm exhausted. I think I can walk but, no, I cannot fly right now."

"Shame," said Mr McAndrew.

"I don't want to give you up," said Myrtle to the angel.

"You tried, Myrtle. That's all that counts. I guess if they've got us surrounded, we should just go out and get it over with."

Myrtle was appalled but even she had run out of ideas. There was no option but to admit defeat so Mr McAndrew opened the potting shed door and they stepped out to meet the policemen.

"There they are!" came a loud cry. Torch beams swung round to find them.

"Yes. That's them!" cried a second voice, which was instantly recognisable as Professor Hoom's.

"Don't hurt them!" shouted a third person.

"That's Isaac's voice," said Myrtle. "They're all here."

"Myrtle! Stay right where you are!" shouted yet another voice.

"That's your mum," said the angel.

"Flipping Nora! Is Nanna here as well?" Myrtle asked and, she may have been imagining it, but she thought she could indeed see the short, wide figure of Nanna waddling around amongst the policemen.

Now that everyone knew where they were, the policemen were closing in rapidly on the potting shed. Mr McAndrew had been right. They were surrounded.

Myrtle took the angel's hand in hers and squeezed it lovingly.

"So this is the end," she said.

Up in the sky, a dozen lights circled around above the allotments.

"Look, they've got helicopters," said Mr McAndrew. "They'd have caught you even if you had managed to fly away."

There was absolutely nowhere for them to run to.

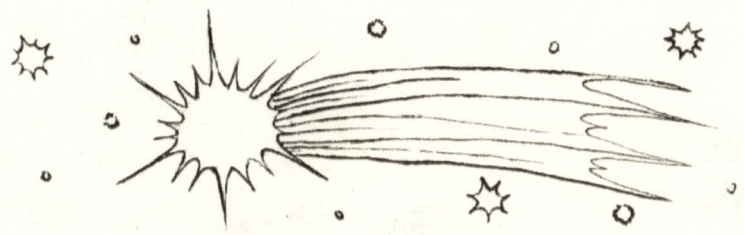

19 – The Company of Angels

And then, quite surprisingly, the angel laughed.

"What is it?" said Myrtle.

The angel faced her, giving her the most joyous smile she had ever seen on his little face.

"Those lights are not helicopters," he said.

Myrtle looked up again at the circling lights.

"Then what are they?" she asked.

"They're my brothers."

By now, the line of people with torches had reached the potting shed and stood around the girl, the angel and Mr McAndrew in a tight semi-circle. There were at least ten policemen. There was Dr Adelman and Isaac. There was Mrs Green and, yes, there was Nanna. And at the very centre of the group was Professor Hoom. He had a strange expression on his face that was partly excitement, partly disgust and really very angry. It was not a nice expression.

"There! There!" he shrieked. "See what I have seen! The boy has wings!"

There were gasps and murmurs amongst the people.

"But that's Bob, isn't it?" said Mrs Green.

"It's an abomination!" screeched Professor Hoom. "Seize it!"

The policemen slowly moved forward but they stopped in their tracks when a loud and powerful voice from above called out, "No!"

Everyone looked up.

The lights in the sky were lower now, growing larger as they came down to the ground. They were angels but not small, child-sized angels like Bob but tall, proud and noble with wings that were each higher and wider than Myrtle's angel friend. They touched down upon the ground, their footsteps as soft and tender as kisses. The haloes of these angels were far more magnificent than the little angel's. The light poured from them, their hair gleaming like precious metals, their eyes glowing like burning coals. Even their skin seemed to shine with warmth and love.

The people gathered round Myrtle and the angel froze in awe and terror. One policeman dropped his torch. Another fled in fear. But the angels paid no attention to them.

The tallest of the angels placed a hand on Bob's shoulder.

"Little brother," he said in deep and warm voice, "It is good to see you."

"And you, Archangel," said Bob, bowing his head.

"We have been looking for you all across the Earth," said the Archangel. "We have missed you keenly. The Celestial City has not been the same without you."

"I've been here with Myrtle," said the little angel. "She looked after me when my wing was hurt."

The Archangel looked directly at Myrtle. His gaze was a beautiful and terrible thing and Myrtle felt like she was a tiny speck of life being stared at through a microscope.

"Then we must offer her our thanks," said the Archangel.

"That's okay," said Myrtle shyly.

"You were hidden from us," the Archangel said to the little angel. "We looked for the glow of your halo but could not find it."

"I was wearing a hat for a lot of the time," said the little angel.

"A hat?"

"A bobble hat," said Myrtle. "A woolly one."

"I see," said the Archangel. "But then, a short while ago, we saw your halo shine, the brightest I have ever seen it and that was how we came to know where you were."

"That was when he was making Belinda all better," said Myrtle. "Belinda's my chicken."

The Archangel raised his eyebrows in interest.

"You used your powers to heal a chicken?"

"Yes," said the little angel.

"You know that we do not interfere in human matters," the Archangel said sternly.

"I know, Archangel."

"I am most displeased."

"But I did what I did out of love," said the little angel.

"And if he hadn't, you would never have seen his halo. You would have never found him," said Myrtle.

"True," said the Archangel.

"And aren't you interfering in human matters just by coming down here?"

The Archangel made a noise that might have been a small chuckle.

"You're quite a bright girl, aren't you?"

The Archangel turned to face the other people: Myrtle's mum and Nanna, Isaac and Dr Adelman, Professor Hoom and the remaining policemen. He stretched out a glowing hand to them.

"Tonight, you will all go home and sleep deeply," he said. "And tomorrow, you will have forgotten all of this. I shall take the memories from you."

The faces of the people showed a variety of expressions. Some, like Mrs Green, were shocked. Some, like Nanna, were just confused. And some, like Dr Adelman, were too entranced to care. But Professor Hoom was none of these things.

"No!" he howled, throwing himself onto his knees. "You can't do this! I refuse to forget!"

"Refuse?" said the Archangel.

"I must know everything about you! I must understand!"

"You don't deserve to understand," said Myrtle angrily. "You wanted to take Bob away. You wanted to lock him up."

"Who's Bob?" said the Archangel.

"That's the name I gave him," explained Myrtle, "because he couldn't tell me his real name."

The little angel suddenly had an idea. He walked up to Professor Hoom as he knelt in the mud.

"Do you want to know something? Do you really want to understand?"

"More than anything," said the professor. "Please!"

And so the angel leant forward so his mouth was right by the professor's ear and, in the tiniest of whispers, the angel told Professor Hoom his real name.

Professor Hoom became absolutely still and, for a moment, Myrtle feared that the little angel had killed him. But then tears sprang to the professor's tiny shiny eyes and he started to make the most peculiar sound. It was a sort of wailing, a sort of barking and a sort of wheezing.

The little angel's real name was a powerful and wondrous thing because it contained nothing but truth. And the absolute truth is something that no human was ever meant to hear because the absolute truth is enough to make a person laugh and cry at the same time.

Which was exactly what Professor Hoom was doing.

And he did not stop.

"So be it," said the Archangel. "We have stayed here too long. It is time to go, little brother."

The little angel turned to Myrtle and gave her a loving hug.

"Thanks for everything, Myrtle."

"Will I ever see you again?" she asked.

"No," said the Archangel. "Even you cannot be allowed to remember. The memory will fade like a dream. It will be as if you two never met."

"I'm going to forget you?" said Myrtle, holding onto the little angel. "But you're my friend. I wished for a friend. I can't lose you."

"You have friends," said the angel, looking over to where Isaac and his uncle stood. "Human ones, as well as chickens. You just need to look. Goodbye, Myrtle."

Without a further word the company of angels, including Bob, flapped their wings and rose up into the air. And as they flew upwards, all the angels began to sing. Their voices intertwined in perfect harmony, weaving a melody that reached right into Myrtle's heart.

It was song without words but Myrtle understood what it meant. It was a song of farewell. It was like the red light of sunset. It was like the falling leaves of autumn. It was like the touch of a goodbye kiss.

There was no song on Earth like it.

Myrtle watched the angels as they flew higher, waving to them even when she knew they couldn't see her. She watched as the lights grew smaller and smaller. She watched until the lights became as faint as the most distant stars. She continued to watch even when they had disappeared altogether.

20 – The Dream

Yawning and stretching, Myrtle awoke. It was morning. Sunlight shone in around the edges of the curtains.

Myrtle had had the most weird and wonderful dreams in the night. As she stared up at her ceiling she tried to remember what the dream had been about. She remembered something about stars and something about a song. There had been a person. A boy? She vaguely remembered golden hair and sparkling blue eyes.

Myrtle tried to remember more but it was like chasing after fog. The more effort she made to hold onto the dream, the more it slipped away from her. Within moments, she was fully awake and the memory of the dream of the boy had gone.

Deep down inside her belly, she felt a little lump of sadness but she did not know why.

But then Myrtle rolled onto her side, put her hand under her pillow and her fingertips brushed against something that in an instant made her little lump of sadness vanish forever.

She pulled the object out and looked at it, hardly daring to believe it was real. It was a feather, as white as a snowflake and as long as Myrtle's hand.

And it was not a chicken feather.